AMY SADLER

# DEAD IS FOR EVER

*Complete and Unabridged*

# LINFORD
*Leicester*

First published in Great Britain in 1997 by
Robert Hale Limited
London

First Linford Edition
published 1999
by arrangement with
Robert Hale Limited
London

British Library CIP Data

Sadler, Amy
    Dead is for ever.—Large print ed.—
    Linford western library
    1. Western stories
    2. Large type books
    I. Title
    823.9'14 [F]

    ISBN 0–7089–5435–9

Published by
F. A. Thorpe (Publishing) Ltd.
Anstey, Leicestershire

Set by Words & Graphics Ltd.
Anstey, Leicestershire
Printed and bound in Great Britain by
T. J. International Ltd., Padstow, Cornwall

This book is printed on acid-free paper

# 1

As he rode along the ridge Sam Carver heard gunfire somewhere below and pulled his horse in behind a piñon. He couldn't tell exactly from where the sound came as the slope was well covered with bushes and young pine trees. He thought that whoever was doing the shooting might well be at the pool where water gathered after it ran down a gully; a place he had used quite a few times.

Someone screamed and Sam's pulse quickened as he recognized it to be that of a female. The pistol firing ceased as he yanked his rifle from its scabbard and reined the horse downward, guiding it expertly between the foliage. The screams sent shivers through Sam as he recalled the last time he'd heard a woman scream so. Two years ago he had come upon an

Arapaho dragging a white woman by the legs over very rough ground. He'd galloped straight at the Indian and knocked him clean off a twenty-foot cliff, sending him plummeting on to a rock in the middle of a river where he'd lain, his back broken. A second Indian had come leaping at him then and slashed across his arm with a knife, but Sam had managed to swing his horse round and give the yelling savage a blow on his back and he'd taken off.

The woman, after he'd eventually got her to talk, said she'd been taken by the Indians after they'd raided their homestead and killed her husband and a hired man. Sam had taken her to the nearest settlement where he'd left her, in a bad state of mind, with a preacher's wife.

The whole thing flashed through Sam's mind as he hurried to the bottom of the slope sending stones rattling before him, which he knew would alert whoever was down there.

Arriving at the bottom he stepped off the horse, leaving him ground-hitched. He moved swiftly through the bushes then came to a halt, listening.

There were two men, at least, he discerned when he heard voices. Sam backed up and moved to his left when he caught sight of a sorrel horse stomping restlessly. Quietly, he levered his Winchester and circled. He saw a covered wagon near a clearing, and a man lying on the ground near it who he assumed was dead. There were some things scattered about next to a smouldering camp fire, and it looked as if someone had been preparing a meal.

A man came out of the trees moving cautiously. 'I'm sure they were dead,' he spoke to another man behind him. His eyes searched around the clearing. Sam moved quickly in behind the wagon.

'Could've been a deer or something, Lew. Let's get the hell away from here. We'll take the girl with us. She can drive the wagon,' the second voice responded.

The first man came to the wagon, still cautious. He stepped over the dead man. The sorrel horse snorted and the others whinnied. He came on round the wagon and let out a startled yell, as Sam Carver swung up the rifle butt, hitting him under the jaw. He slumped against the wagon and slid to the ground. Carver dragged him away quickly and left him under a bush.

Jake Bradowski went and fetched the girl from the bushes, where he'd dragged her before he'd heard the stones rattling. She cowered and shivered in terror and shock. She had no doubts about what her fate would be with these two vile creatures. If she could just get to the sorrel, she might have a chance of getting away. She suddenly pulled away but Bradowski hit her hard across the face and she yelped with pain.

'Come on you, don't give me no trouble. I got plans for you, missy,'

Bradowski snarled. 'Where the hell is Lew?' he muttered. He heard a sound over at the wagon. He let go of the girl, drawing his pistol.

Hope Bennett was no weakling, she seized her chance and turning took off. Bradowski whirled and sprang after her, grabbing at her dress, tearing it, as he swung her round and up against him. His liquored breath caused Hope to turn her head away.

'I said, you behave,' Bradowski shouted at her, running his hand over her buttocks.

The first bullet from Carver's rifle swept past the outlaw's face and he let go of the girl hurriedly, a look of surprise crossing his face as he got off a shot with his sidegun. The second shot took him in the left lung. He gasped as his finger pulled the trigger again but the bullet went wide of Carver, whose third shot hit him in the solar plexus. He slumped to his knees, dropping the Colt, and clutched at his belly, 'Oh! Jeez-us!' he spluttered, as Carver advanced. 'Who the hell are you?'

'I'm justice, you mean sonofabitch,' said Carver, and spat into the ground. He turned the dying man on to his side, 'What name shall I put on your marker, you piece of horse-dung?' Sam asked.

Bradowski's face was full of pain. Blood oozed from his middle and upper chest. He opened his mouth, but nothing but blood came forth.

'Miss, I'll be back in a minute,' Carver turned to the girl who was standing in shock, her eyes staring down at Bradowski, then looking after the other big man and wondering from where her rescuer had come.

Lew Daggett was coming round and on hearing footsteps his hand moved to his holster belt; his pistol was gone. His thoughts were bitter. Neither he nor Jake had seen anyone else with the man and woman, the girl and the guide, so where had this one come from? He felt the strong hand yank him out by his coat collar, as he made to get up. A

6

rifle dug into his ribs. If only he could grab it.

'Don't try anything or you'll get what your sidekick got. Walk slowly to the wagon,' Sam told him. He could see the man was fairly stocky, likely in his thirties, dark hair and black angry eyes. 'Girl, you get some rope and bring it here,' he called out to Hope who had come to look at the dead man by the wagon. Without a word she climbed into the wagon and came out with what was probably a clothesline. He could see tears on her cheeks, as she handed it to him.

'Put your hands behind your back,' Carver told the glowering man, whose breath exuded liquor.

Daggett did as he was told. He could see Bradowski lying some yards away. Well, it didn't seem like this fella intended killing him. Best he bide his time. The dark would come soon and then there might be a chance to get away. He still had his knife down his boot.

After Carver had tied Daggett securely to the wagon wheel and taken a look at his sidekick, making sure he was dead, he brought in his own horse, collected the outlaws' horses and tied them, including the sorrel, on a line strung from the wagon to a tree. He unhitched the wagon horses, stripped them of the harness and took them to drink at the watering hole, then tied them on the line. The chore done he turned his attention to the girl. She was nowhere in sight. 'Damn!' Sam swore. Then suddenly she came from the far side of the clearing running, her eyes red, her face swollen from the blow Jake Bradowski had given her. When he got to her she began to sob uncontrollably.

'Listen,' he said, feeling awkward. 'It's coming dark so we'd best stay here until morning. I'll get the fire going and make some coffee first. That dead man by the wagon, was he your father?' he asked gently. 'Was there just the two of you?'

'No, he wasn't. His name was Will Shannon, our guide. Back there,' she pointed, letting out a racking sob, 'Mr Morris and his wife. They were gathering wood when those two came out of the bushes. The dead one killed them, and then grabbed me. Will got off two shots before that one shot him,' she pointed at Daggett.

'I'll be taking him to Vernon, the sheriff there will hang the bas — Sorry miss,' Carver apologized. 'I'll go bring them in, could be cougar about,' he said grimly.

While Carver brought in the two bodies, placing them with Shannon's and covering them with a tarpaulin he found tied on the wagon, Hope got the fire going, wondering anxiously what was to become of her now. The man tied up was watching her and it scared her. If he should get loose . . . She shivered.

Carver was looking angry. When he'd found the woman who lay on her back, her clothing badly torn, her face

9

had an expression of shock on it, the eyes staring. 'I'll bury them tomorrow when it comes light,' he told Hope.

He saw the girl had somehow got herself together and seemed to be coping. It was best she busy herself after what she'd been through. He would like to put a bullet in the outlaw who sat watching them with an air of nonchalance. He'd need to be careful with that one.

It was not Sam's way though to kill out of hand. Let the law take care of him. Thank God he'd been too young to take part in that awful Civil War when people did such bad things, excusing themselves it was the war.

By the time dark came the girl had produced from the wagon some antelope meat and beans, which Sam heated. She ate little and Sam didn't press her. He didn't press her about anything except her name, and those of the others and where they'd been heading for. She'd had enough to cope with for one day. He figured she was about sixteen, but had observed she seemed mature. After washing herself at the pool and putting on a fresh skirt, Sam was surprised to find himself staring at her. She'd brushed her light-brown hair, and he suddenly found heat going through him. The type of women he'd been keeping company with the past few years had never given him such quick-jerk reaction as this young thing had. Guilt swept through Sam. The sooner he got her to where she could be looked after, the better. She must have relatives somewhere, surely? Vernon, though, was not a place for a young girl such as her.

Lew Daggett was given coffee and food. He was allowed his hands free while he ate but was still tied tightly to the wagon. He had noted the man's awkwardness with the girl and his covert appraisal of her after she had put on fresh clothes. Jake and he would surely have fought over her if this fella hadn't come along. Jake had most likely enjoyed the woman

11

before he'd killed her. He was gone for some time and had scratches on his face when he came out of the timber. Coping with the guide and settling the wagon horses, he'd been too busy, then the stones had come down the slope.

He must get away somehow in the night. This man who'd told the girl he was Sam Carver, was no fool. It'd be hard to put a tag on him. Probably in his late twenties, strong built, and good looking. He might even be a lawman, or could be ex-military. He had given Lew, while tying him up, a look of pure condemnation. The girl seemed to be trusting him for sure. Then what else could she do? They hadn't said a lot, and had spoken low during the meal.

If he could just get at his knife when they weren't watching, it wouldn't take long to cut himself free. If he only managed to get his ankles free, and away from the wagon, he could ride with his hands tied. Another thought came to Daggett. If he did get away, he could dry-gulch them and take the girl. He would not have Bradowski to deal with now. He could claim she was his wife, she could be useful. Yeah, he could keep her awhile then taken her to Carlos d'Angelo over in Shreveport who would pay a good price for her, and take her to New Orleans for the rich fellas. Daggett ran his tongue round his lips. He could get a fair price for the horses and wagon too. 'Hey, fella! You got a stogey — mebbe a bottle? It's sure gonna be cold; a long night,' he called over to Carver.

Carver got up and lit a thin cheroot, and walking over gave it to Daggett, sticking it into his mouth. 'Get some sleep,' he said, checked the ropes and strode to one of the horses and brought back a slicker and put it around the outlaw. Why he should bother with such scum he couldn't say.

'Best bed down in the wagon, miss, it will be cold tonight. I'll wake you first light, and then I'll bury your friends, have some breakfast and then head on out for Vernon. It's a rough place but there's a rooming-house I know, run by a decent woman. It'd be best you go back where you came from. It is no good for a female on her own out here. Not unless she's — well, you know,' Sam said blushing.

'I can't go back. I have no place to go to,' Hope said tremulously.

'Lord, girl! Where were you going with the Morrises?' Sam asked, exasperatedly. 'What were they to you?'

'They took care of me after I ran off from an orphanage. I have an uncle in Denver. He sent money to them but I haven't heard from him for almost a year.' Hope broke off.

'Your parents, where are they?' Sam asked her.

'Dead! They were drowned when the ship bringing us from England ran on to some rocks off Maine. I was only three then. My uncle saved me, but he couldn't take care of me, so he took me to an orphanage in Baltimore. The Morrises worked there, then later they left to work for some rich folks. I was about twelve when I ran away and found them. Later we moved to Vicksburg.'

'Did they treat you all right?'

'Well, I had to work hard, and they were quite strict and religious. They got a letter from some old friends telling them it was good in Denver, so they decided to go there, especially as that was the last place Uncle Matt wrote from.'

'They could have got a train there from Kansas City,' Carver said suspiciously.

'Mr Morris said it was too much money and he wanted to bring some things along. Will Shannon said he wouldn't charge for guiding us as he was going there anyway. The Morrises needed a rest and they thought it would be very interesting. Will kept us laughing with his tales. He shot game for us. He taught me to drive the wagon and to ride and shoot.'

'I see,' said Carver, though he

thought the Morrises had not been too smart, nor Shannon, as there still were Indians about. Perhaps the sheriff in Vernon could find out if her uncle was still in Denver. Tomorrow he'd get her and the outlaw bastard, whose name he would not say, to town.

# 2

When Carver heard Daggett fidgeting for some time, he got up and went to check on him. He could see the rope had slackened at the wheel so he drew the man's arms up tighter to the spoke.

'It's damned cold,' Daggett said crossly.

'You shouldn't have killed those folks, then you'd have been into a settlement for the night,' Carver answered him angrily. He put more wood on the fire and got back under his blanket, drawing his rifle in close.

When dawn came, Carver got up and stamped around a few moments, checked on his prisoner, then took a spade from the side of the wagon and went to find a soft spot by some trees and started digging. He dug one long grave for the Morrisses and Shannon, and a separate one for the outlaw.

Hope was up and cooking breakfast when Sam came for the bodies. She handed him a mug of coffee.

'Did you sleep?' he asked her. She seemed well composed, though her face was swollen and wore a strained look on it. It was hardly surprising, he thought.

'A little,' she said. 'Shouldn't we have taken them to town?' she asked anxiously.

'It's not much of a place and the undertaker would charge about seven bucks apiece for the coffins. You'll be needing money. I'd best check their pockets,' Sam said uneasily. 'Have they got relatives anywhere?'

'I don't think so. Well, Mr Morris had a brother in England, but I don't know where. They had friends up in Denver. I can check through their papers,' Hope said.

'If they were your guardians then you'll be almost like a daughter and could claim what they had. There's also the guide's horse and gear. The sheriff in Vernon will take everything he can get his hands on. You let me deal with things. I'll think up something. First I'll take that creature to the sheriff,' Sam told her sympathetically. Lord knows what would happen to the girl.

To Sam's surprise, there was a roll of $2,000 in a leather pouch around Morris's neck; he put it into his jacket pocket. He'd give it to her later. He took the gold rings off their fingers and a silver locket from the woman's neck and gave them to Hope. Shannon had sixty dollars, his timepiece and guns. The outlaw forty dollars and his guns. Sheriff Bowers would claim those and the horses, he was thinking.

Daggett, who was watching closely, was furious that he had not been able to get to his knife. That bastard was helping himself to what there was. He'd be after the girl next.

Hope came to the back of the wagon and got up into it. 'If I was you, missy, I'd watch that two-bit, four-flusher.

He'll dump you and take everything. You don't know who he is. You hear me?' he called to her as Carver took away the woman wrapped in a sheet.

Hope came down from the wagon. 'You shut up! You murdering scum. You're lucky he didn't shoot you too,' she snapped.

Daggett sneered. 'Jest you wait, he'll have you. He ain't no better than Bradowski. He's jest more cunning!'

Hope flushed and walked away. Supposing he was right? Well, she had Bert Morris's Colt and a box of ammo, hidden in her own case of belongings. She'd be keeping a close watch on them both.

By the time Carver had buried the bodies, said a few words over them and burned out the names of the Morrises on a piece of wood, placing it at the grave, he was sweating and ready for food. An hour later they were moving out. Sam had the outlaw on a close lead rein while Hope drove the wagon with the two spare mounts tied behind. When Carver complimented her on how she handled the wagon horses, she was pleased. 'I see you're no greenhorn,' he told her.

'Bert taught me,' she replied, flushing deeply.

They had been moving steadily along the trail for about an hour through timbered terrain when Daggett made his move. Carver had tied his right hand to the pommel, leaving his left free to handle the reins. He didn't know that Daggett was ambidextrous. Lew slid his left hand into his long boot and drew out the knife. In a flash he had cut the lead rein, swung his horse round and got to the rear. He was up into the wagon before Hope knew what had happened, and had a hand to her mouth, the other holding the knife at her throat. She let out a scream as Daggett shouted at Carver — who had whipped round, his Colt in his hand. 'You drop the gun, or I'll slit her throat. You know I will.'

The wagon horses came to a halt and

exchanged playful nips with each other. Carver was in no doubt that the man meant it. He dropped his Colt and sat still, bitterly chastising himself for not searching him more thoroughly.

'Get down quick,' Daggett told him, still holding the knife at Hope's throat. 'Move away from the horse.'

Sam did as he was told. He daren't make a move for his rifle, on the horse. The bastard could slash the girl's throat in a second.

Daggett forced Hope down, keeping close in behind her, and walked her towards Carver's horse. Quickly he pulled the rifle from its scabbard and levered it. He pushed the girl away roughly and fired at Carver. Sam, who'd anticipated the move, dived, but the bullet burned across his temple before he rolled under a bush. He lay still as Daggett came and looked down at him. Daggett whirled round when he heard the girl streaking to the rear of the wagon. He got to her fast as she tried to get one of the horses. 'No you don't,' he growled at her.

'Is he dead?' Hope asked fearfully, shaking all over. Her fate was sealed now. This man would show her no mercy. Even if she could get away, she had no one now.

'Girl, you go get that other horse and bring it here. Don't try to ride off. I could drop you in a flash. You better learn to do as I say, and be quick.'

Carver tried to get up but went dizzy and passed out. Hope took his horse and tied it with the others. Daggett mounted his own, telling her to drive on. He held the rifle across his lap pointed at her, so there was nothing she could do. If only she could get at the Colt she'd hidden away. She felt extremely upset about Carver, who'd stopped to help then paid with his life.

Daggett was feeling pleased with himself, but he must get off the main trail and find a place to hide awhile. He could sell the spare horses, and enjoy the girl. He should have gone through that bastard's pockets. Well, there was no going back now. The sun was well up and there would be others moving along the trail. When he saw a fork off the trail, he told the girl to turn into what looked to be an old, grown-over track. It was rough going for a mile or two then suddenly they came to a clearing where an old shack stood at the edge of the trees. Daggett grinned. This would do. He could see a creek not far away and heard ducks.

After backing the wagon in under the trees, he took Hope with him to inspect the cabin. The roof was still intact, and there was an old stove and a bunk bed with a mildewed mattress upon it, which looked as if some animal had been using it. It would do for what he had in mind. Anyway, they would sleep in the wagon. His tongue ran round his mouth in anticipation. He figured the shack was too far away from the trail for anyone to notice smoke, and it was unlikely they'd come to investigate.

'You start gathering wood. We'll fix

us some food,' Daggett ordered Hope. 'That fella sure was stingy with what he gave me yesterday. Well, I sure fixed him. Wonder who the hell he was?' Daggett said, then he guffawed loudly.

'Might have been a lawman,' Hope said angrily. 'They'll be looking for you, after they find him.'

Daggett gave her a scornful look. 'You can forget him. He was nobody. Jest a trail-bum. Now I'm gonna take care of you. You'll do as I say. Anyone asks, you're my wife, see. You'll enjoy it. Yes, by God, Lew Daggett has a real way with wimen,' he bragged.

Hope went outside into the trees. So, that was his name. One she would not be likely to forget. He would not be the first man to force himself upon her. The manager at the orphanage, after the Morrises had left, had done that; told her he would kill her if she told anyone. That's when she had run away and found Helen and Bert Morris, who'd taken care of her then. Even

Bert Morris had sometimes looked at her in the way men often did. She knew she was attractive, and had learned to recognize that certain look some men gave her. Sam Carver had sweated after she had changed her clothing and tidied herself. But Sam had been kind, and she had been drawn to him. She had never before felt so strange about a man. If only that sonofabitch Daggett hadn't shot him. What if a coyote or cougar got at Sam? She wanted to cry, but she couldn't anymore. That awful man, Bradowski, must have defiled poor Helen Morris. She had been too trusting, too religious. If she could hear Hope now using profane language, she'd turn in her grave. Well, she was on her own now. She must look after herself, the best way she could.

★ ★ ★

Sam Carver stirred as he felt the rain running down his face. Slowly he pulled himself up and put a hand

26

to his temple, which was throbbing. His fingers came away red from the groove. 'Well, I'll be damned! I'm still alive!' he muttered. He moved away from the trees and got back on to the trail. There was no sign of the wagon. Then he didn't really expect there would be. Where would that rotten piece of humanity have taken the girl? He'd not dare go into Vernon. Would he ravage her then kill her? He would get a fair price for the wagon and all the horses, and whatever else was in there. Oh damn! Why was I such a fool? I always searched my bounty prisoners for knives. The whole damned thing took me by surprise, Sam excused himself. The girl would be better off dead than being with a man such as that.

Sam stumbled on something and saw it was his own pistol. That was something, he still had bullets in the holster belt. He looked up at the sky and saw it was grey all round. The rain wasn't heavy but he would be plenty wet by the time he reached Vernon. About eight miles away, he reckoned, as he set off to walk, somewhat unsteadily.

An hour later, Sam rode into Vernon atop the stage that had pulled up and given him a lift, for which he was thankful. He was also thankful that the outlaw had not thought to search his pockets after shooting him. Too much of a hurry to get off with the girl.

After Sam had been and apprised Sheriff Bowers of what had occurred at Walter's Spring, he went to the store and bought a new set of clothes, then had a soak at the bath-house, after which he got a room at Annie's where he partook of a huge breakfast before going to bed. He was out like a light in no time.

When Sam got up next morning, having slept almost twenty-four hours, he let Annie put some iodine on his wound. Sam was one of her favourites, though she didn't really hold with bounty-hunters. 'Has anyone come into town either yesterday or this morning with some horses for sale?' he asked her. 'Might be a young girl with the fella.'

'Not as I've heard. Duke Carling might know. He buys horses. One of your warranties you been chasing, gone an' took your horse?' Annie asked, amused. Her smile faded as Sam looked peeved. Sam did do the country a service. He was an honest man, a durned sight more than Bowers. He never got off his ass unless there was something in it for him.

When Sam went back to see the sheriff about the reward for Bradowski, whom he had seen a likeness to on a poster, Bowers said there was no reward without a body or proof. 'The girl will be dead by now. That devil will kill her after he's amused himself with her. You know that, don't you?' he said to Carver, without a hint of sympathy.

Sam, feeling frustrated, said, 'Well, somebody should try and find that wagon and that fella Lew. I don't know his other name. He wouldn't say. I can dig up the other one and bring him in, or you can send Deputy Toliver with me. He ain't doing nothing but making sheep's-eyes at Beth Thomson in Autry's store.'

Bowers gave Sam a thoughtful look. 'All right! You can take Tolly and show him the corpse. If he says it's anything like the poster, you can have the $500. You should have put a slug in that other one right away. He'd done murder, so you say.'

'Yeah, well, I regret that now,' said Sam.

Before Sam left with Deputy Toliver, after he'd bought himself another horse, he sent off a telegraph to the sheriff's office in Denver, enquiring about a Matthew Bennett. An answer came back two days later while Sam was away, saying there wasn't anyone of that name in Denver, so far as they could discover. It had not occurred to Sam that Hope's uncle might not be a Bennett but was, in fact, her late mother's brother and was Matthew Freeman.

## 3

The weather was still inclined to rain as Deputy Toliver, who was not well pleased, rode out with Sam Carver for Walter's Spring. Carver rode a deep tan horse that had cost him $120 with saddle. He'd also had to purchase a Winchester rifle for $150, as Daggett had taken his other one. Riding fairly quickly they reached the water hole in two hours. Carver immediately set about digging up Bradowski's corpse with a spade he'd brought along. After taking a good look at the body, Toliver said he was sure it was the outlaw. He wanted to get back as quickly as possible.

'Good,' said Sam. 'I'll give you a hundred of the reward.' He was figuring to keep Toliver amenable. He had the money he'd taken off the Morrises and Shannon. He would give

Bowers a few bucks, saying it was what he took off Bradowski and Shannon, and make out that the Morrises' dough was still on the wagon with the girl. If he found her he would give that to her. 'We'll go now to where I was shot and try and track the wagon,' he told the deputy.

'I reckon them folks wasn't too bright. Could be that guide was in with them two. Wouldn't be the first time folks got misled,' Toliver said sagely.

'According to the girl, Shannon was taken on from the start. He tried to shoot one of 'em, but they got him first. Could have been trailing 'em for one or two days, is my guess,' said Sam.

They rode on in silence and arrived at the place Carver had been shot. It was darkening and the sky was heavy with rain clouds. 'We'll not find their tracks this day,' said Toliver grouchily.

'I know where there's a cave. We can

use it tonight and start again in the morning,' Carver said determinedly.

* * *

Lew Daggett took the wood from Hope and dropped it on the floor by the stove. He shook the piping and debris fell down it. He opened the front and pushed the wood inside and soon had the fire going. 'What have you got in the wagon?' he asked Hope.

'Not much. Some beans and side-bacon, only it will be off now. There's coffee beans, flour and sugar, and a few tins of fruit. Why don't you give me one of the horses and let me go?' she implored him.

Daggett looked at her in surprise. 'Now why would I want to do that? Tonight, girlee, you and me's going to be real cosy in that wagon. I sure do wish we had a bottle.'

'I don't drink,' Hope snapped. 'I'll go get the food.' She walked out through the door. Dare she try to

34

make a run for it? If she could just get to the sorrel.

Daggett watched her go, a leer on his face. Part of the pleasure with a one like her was the anticipation. She seemed to have accepted her fate, he thought. What he'd give for some whiskey. Hell, he hadn't searched Bradowski's saddle-bags. He started running. Christ! He'd left the rifles on the horses.

The horses were already cropping grass near the trees. Hope hesitated, then she heard Daggett coming. It wasn't the time. She got up into the wagon and reached for a box and hauled it out. 'You'd better carry it,' she told him as he came up, red in the face.

Daggett took the box. 'You go first,' he told her. 'I don't want you pulling no tricks. You try getting one of them horses, I'll run you down. I can outride anybody on Swifty. We've won races at fairs.'

Then I'll know which one to take, Hope thought. The rain was falling and she thought of Sam Carver's body laid under those bushes where a coyote or cougar could get at him. She let out a sob as she took the things out of the box.

'You get the food ready, I'm going to see to the wagon and the horses. I'll have to hobble them so they can graze.'

After he'd seen to the horses, he took the rifles and hid them under some bushes. He found some spare clothing in Shannon's saddle-bag, and beef jerky in Bradowski's, and a pair of shoes. In the wagon he saw a trunk with sheets and clothing in it. There was a small box with some cheap jewellery inside it and a few letters. He heard a noise and swung round. 'Don't you ever come up on me again like that,' he shouted at Hope. 'I could've shot you!'

'So,' she said, 'you'd be doing me a favour. I've got nothing to live for now. Supper's ready. Pass me those plates in that tub,' Hope snapped.

Flushing deeply, Daggett picked up

the tub and got down. Sooner I'm rid of her, he was thinking, the better. It won't be no fun if that's how she's gonna be. No fun at all!

Hope was thinking she must get to the gun she'd hidden before he found it, and hide it some other place. Could she kill Daggett, though, if she did get the chance? Shooting at tins was one thing, but at a live person . . . ?

After the meal was finished Hope got up off the rickety chair. 'I'll go get more water from the creek,' she said, and taking a wooden bucket, went quickly over to the creek and filled it. Back at the shack she put a large pan on the stove and filled it and turned to leave again.

'Where you going?' Daggett asked suspiciously.

'I want a towel and some soap. I'm going to have a wash. You can get out. We'll be needing more wood,' Hope told him, not feeling as confident as she sounded.

Daggett grinned. 'Yeah, you make

yourself real nice. I like my wimen to smell good,' he told Hope.

'I'm not your woman, and you stink like an animal. If you cleaned yourself up you might look halfway decent,' Hope flung at him and got out fast, amazed at her temerity.

Daggett was confused. One minute she was cold as ice, the next almost as if she really wanted him. He got off the bunk and from his saddle-bag he'd dumped on the floor, he took a piece of soap and rumpled towelling, then strode off to the creek. Maybe she'd come to her senses, figured it was better to go along with him. She was probably starved of a man's company. Them bible-toting folks would have kept a close eye on her, though there was something about her that told him she was no innocent. His heart thumped as he took off his shirt and sluiced his neck and face, shuddering.

Hope opened her case, which held her few possessions. Quickly she took her towel and wrapped the pistol in it. Will Shannon had given her a few lessons with it. 'You never know, miss, what you meet on the trail,' he'd told her. 'It ain't no use if you don't know how to use it.' After some practice she had managed to hit the tins he set up. She went back to the shack, taking the lantern with her. The dark was descending. She could hear Daggett whistling on his way back from the creek, and pushed the Colt under the old mattress. The door burst open. 'I'm not washed yet,' she told him, anxiously.

'Aw, come on now! You sharpen up! I'm washed and you know what I want. You can make it easy on yourself. Either way, I'm not waiting much longer. It'd be more comfortable in the wagon under the blankets,' Daggett said coaxingly.

'I've got to wash first. I told you I need hot water. I won't take long,' Hope replied, playing for time.

'I'll be waiting for you, so you be sensible, and don't even think of trying to run. I'd catch you and beat you good, you hear me?' said Daggett and left. 'Oh Christ! I wish I was in Mexico with a couple of *putas* and a bottle of tequila,' he muttered as he got up into the wagon, where he took off his boots and pants and got under the blankets on a feather eiderdown.

Using the heated water, Hope sponged herself all over after dropping her clothes. It felt so good. She had not had a chance for days to wash herself properly. The shack was quite warm. If only it didn't smell so. She dried herself then put more wood into the stove and reached for her stockings. She was pulling on her bodice when the door burst open and Daggett stood there staring as she covered herself hastily, almost giggling at the sight of Lew Daggett wearing only his long johns, boots and shirt.

'Holy shit!' he said. 'You sure got one hell of a figure! You sure do take your time, girl!' He turned and slammed the door shut, shaking the wall.

Hope screamed as he came towards her, then turned and grabbed the Colt from under the mattress, pulling the hammer back. 'Don't come near me, you murdering scum,' she yelled at him.

Daggett stood still, fury in his eyes. 'Where in hell you get that Colt?' He took a step forward, a grin on his face. 'You ain't going to shoot nobody with that, it ain't got no bullets in it,' he tried bluffing her.

Hope squeezed the trigger and Daggett was slammed back into the wall as the bullet hit him in the throat.

'You damned . . . ' he spluttered as blood ran from his mouth. He tried to get to Hope.

Hope's hands shook as she fired again, twice, and he hit the floor with a thump, barely missing the stove, and lay still.

Hope sank on to the bunk and sat there, her whole frame shaking, staring at Daggett. She had killed him. Oh God, what else should she have done? He would not have spared her. After a while she got up, a grim determination in her as she opened the door. The clouds were gone and she could see stars twinkling overhead. The fool thought I'd let him defile me. Well, he surely found out the hard way. 'Sam, wherever you are, and Will, too. Rest in peace 'cos I got that sonofabitch, and now I'm free of him,' she told the sky, and breathed in deeply. What would the Morrises think of her profanity, she wondered?

After dragging Daggett outside and into the timber she threw out the filthy mattress, went and fetched the quilt and blankets and made herself comfortable. She felt safer in the shack. After building up the stove she lay down. She had killed a man. Had seen the shocked surprise on his face, then the anger. He'd deserved to die. She felt no pity for Daggett. Very soon she fell into deep sleep.

The morning was fresh and clear and the nickering horses woke Hope. She got off the bunk hurriedly. They had somehow got themselves tangled up so she got them sorted out and tied on a line. How on earth was she going to manage them all? Well, first things first. It was just daybreak and she was ravenously hungry. There was flour and she made some sourdough bread like Helen Morris had taught her. She must get to a store. Vernon was the place Sam had been taking them to.

The birds were singing and a squirrel ran up a tree. There were wild ducks fluttering about at the creek. Suddenly, Hope felt wonderfully alive. The sun was up and she was free. If she went into Vernon to try and sell the horses, someone might recognize his horse. Would anyone believe her story? It was a risk. She must have money though. Daggett, he would have some on him, yes. She rushed into the trees, then turned back. His pants

43

and jacket would be in the wagon. Quickly, she got up inside. She found what appeared to be an army paybook in a pocket of the jacket. Lord, what if they were looking for him? She found a wallet and fifty-five dollars in it. She grinned. In the pants pockets there was a dirty handkerchief, and three dollars and two bits. Now she could buy supplies. If she sold the wagon, all the horses and whatever else there was, she could buy a ticket to Denver on a stagecoach, and go find Uncle Matthew. What if he's not there now?

As Hope sat drinking coffee, she pondered her fate. The money would run out eventually, no matter how careful she was. If she took a job with some rich folks, it would be like before. Groping hands and no one to protect her. The more she thought about things, the more she was convinced that her uncle had not really wanted her. Perhaps he'd married. He would have someone, he always had liked women, and liquor. Most men who'd been to sea were like that.

Misery and hopelessness swept over Hope. Sam had said the sheriff at Vernon wasn't too honest. Whoever bought the wagon and horses would be sure to give her as little as possible, of that she was sure. The sheriff would probably take everything and have her sent to one of those places for the homeless, or, she didn't like to think of the alternatives. I'll stay here a day or two and think things out. I can get a deer, or a duck. There were the rifles, too, and side-arms of Will and Bradowski, not to mention Daggett's.

First Hope searched the wagon but found only his Colt and rifle. She looked about for almost an hour before she found the rifles under a bush. She giggled inanely. She could get a fair price for them, surely. She knew how to cut hair. What if she opened up a barber's shop? Why the hell not? Perhaps back in Wichita Springs, that had seemed a nice place, as she recalled. By God, I'll do something. I'm not gonna be licked, she told herself with conviction, and went off skipping towards the creek.

# 4

After finishing breakfast, Carver and Toliver left the cave. Sam felt better now he'd caught up on his sleep. Toliver, however, wasn't overly cheerful. 'We ain't going to find them now,' he said sourly, as they rode down to the trail. 'If we don't find any sign of the wagon by this afternoon, I'm heading back,' he told Sam.

'Well, at least we'll've tried. They might've turned back eastwards. There's no way of knowing,' Sam replied. 'Wagons and stage-coaches pass along here regularly. I guess nobody could say who or what's been over the trail these last few days. We could try one or two of the homesteads, and ask if anyone has seen a wagon with horses aback of it.'

'Yeah, that's about all we can do,' Toliver agreed.

Carefully, they rode back westwards, Toliver pausing often to use his field-glasses, sweeping the terrain. They made a detour to a homestead about two miles from the track, but Ned Rawlins, the farmer, said he hadn't noticed a wagon with four spare horses. Returning to the trail, entering it way past the spot where Daggett had turned off, Sam and Toliver missed seeing the wheel indentations, though most of the hoofmarks and ruts were now filled with rain water.

Carver stopped and questioned everyone they met on the trail, but no one was of any help to them.

By late afternoon, Toliver said he was calling the search off, but Sam said he would carry on. 'You tell Bowers about Bradowski, and you don't have to say I'm giving you a hundred bucks. An' make sure he applies for the reward,' he urged the deputy.

Toliver said he would see to it, and took off at a gallop down the trail.

It did seem rather hopeless, Sam

admitted to himself. Guilt ran through him. He was relieved that they had not come across the girl's body anywhere. She could, though, have been hidden or buried, if she had been killed, where no one would ever find her. He surely had bungled things, though he'd been very tired when it had all happened so unexpectedly. A couple of miles further along, Sam took a track that was not much used, but thought it was worthwhile taking a look. They might well be gone past Vernon by now. That fiend, Lew, would find a place to hide the wagon, then amuse himself with the girl. He might have run out of liquor by now, and that was one thing that might have him seek a store, and they'd need food too. They had plenty to sell. If only he had an idea which way they'd headed, Sam wished, miserably.

At the time Carver was searching the brakes near a river, Hope Bennett was sitting by the creek enjoying the late summer sunshine, and admiring the leaves which were already turning. She had busied herself all morning. First, she had dug a grave and buried the outlaw, a gruesome task, which had tired her out. After a rest, she then cleaned out the wagon and burnt most of the Morrises' clothing, keeping only two blouses, a shirt and good suit, the bed clothing and table linen. These, she thought, would come in handy. She also cleaned out the shack and took across a folding chair for her use. Hope had no idea how long she'd be staying. It was such a lovely place. Just to be able to do as she pleased was a whole new exciting adventure for her.

One thing Hope needed was food, and as the daylight began to fade, she took up Shannon's Winchester, put in some shells and went into the timber. It was not long before she saw some antelopes heading over to the creek, and very quietly she levered the gun. Slipping from tree to tree, she stalked them, and when within fifty yards she lifted the rifle, took careful aim and squeezed the trigger. She almost fell backwards as the antelopes leapt away across the creek, then to her amazement, one stumbled, fell and lay kicking. Throwing off her shoes and lifting her skirt, Hope waded across the creek, the water almost up to her thighs. She felt sick when she looked down at the poor animal as it lay gasping. There was blood on its side and oozing from its mouth. It gave one last kick and lay still.

Hope tried to lift the animal but found it rather heavy. 'Damn!' she swore, then ran to the creek and waded back across to fetch the sorrel. Back again at the deer, she pulled the sorrel down and managed to get the dead creature across its rump, then carefully she held it there while the horse got up again, snorting its disapproval, though it was used to carrying game.

After dropping the antelope off by the shack, Hope fetched the knife that had belonged to Lew, and cut into the hide the way she had watched Will Shannon do it, and did the best she could, grimacing and almost throwing up. Now she had food for a while, but it would have been nice had there been some potatoes and greens to go with it.

During the next days the weather became cooler. Hope was well aware that she must be moving on soon. On the third day she had gone across the creek and seen a lot of cattle grazing, and two riders, away in the distance. She decided it was best she left the shack before someone came asking questions. She felt it would be best to go during the night. The moon was almost full, and she would like to get through Vernon while folks were asleep. The thought of the sheriff, or someone else, sending her off to one of those institutions, or whatever, literally terrified her. Never again was she going to be ordered around, or molested. Never! A gut instinct told her she must avoid that place.

When she had made more space in the wagon, Hope put all the saddles inside. Then she tethered all the spare horses at the rear of the wagon. They were, more or less, used to one another now, but still often exchanged playful nips. Once they were moving, they settled down. The moon was up and a soft wind blew in her face as Hope gave all her attention to handling the reins. She surely had learned a lot since leaving Vicksburg. It seemed a hell of a long time ago. The horses, having been well rested, kept up a good pace and were happy to be on the move. Hope was surprised how soon they came to Vernon, where she saw the name on a livery barn. As Sam had said, it wasn't much of a place. A large sign drew her attention, which said that the railroad lines would soon be coming to Vernon. Only a dog barked as she drove the wagon out at the far end of the main street. Hope breathed a sigh of relief.

There were fewer trees, Hope noticed, and she could see the plains stretching for miles. She had no idea of the time because Bert Morris's timepiece had run down, and Carver had not given her a key when he'd handed it to her. She thought, wistfully, how nice it would be had they been journeying together to take up land somewhere, and set down roots. She jerked her thoughts back to reality as a coyote howled somewhere in the plain. The horses behind made startled noises, so she pulled up, got down and went back to check they were still tied securely, and to draw some comfort from them. They were all she had. 'You all behave now,' she told them, giving them a reassuring pat. Getting the two wagon horses harnessed up and lifting the wagon tongue had been difficult for her. It would be best to be rid of it as soon as she could. She would keep Sam's and Will's horses as she had a strong bond with them now, and couldn't bear to think they might be treated harshly by new owners. A faint hint of dawn broke in the east, but Hope was unaware of this as her head dropped on to her chest and she slumped back against a chest of drawers.

★ ★ ★

Jan Sprague halted his roan horse at the edge of the trees. He pulled a spyglass from a saddle-bag and sat quietly observing the scene. When he saw the wagon tilted precariously on the bank at the creek, he was puzzled. At the rear of it were four horses, obviously tied, or they'd be at the water like the two wagon horses. Putting the spyglass away, he reined his horse down the slope. Whoever was with that wagon was mighty careless. Might be drunk or wounded, he thought.

As Sprague came cautiously in at the rear of the wagon, he dismounted, drew his Colt and walked past the nickering horses, now moving about restlessly. He still could see no one so he stepped up on the foothold at the front. 'My-oh-my!' he uttered, in surprise. What he saw was a body propped against a chest, a floppy hat across the face. Gently, he lifted the hat and again was surprised. It was a female, a young one, and quite a looker. Her light-brown hair had fallen across her face. With relief Jan saw that she was breathing, in fact had fallen asleep. What in tarnation is a girl like her doing out here, all on her lonesome? Jan wondered. As far as he could see, anyway. 'Hey, miss,' he prodded her. 'Wake up.' He shook her shoulder. Hope awoke with a start. Something had touched her. She opened her eyes and was held in paralysis for one or two seconds, before she let out a scream.

Sprague pulled back. 'Whoa there! I ain't agoing to hurt you. Miss, you better get down and move this wagon before it tips into the creek,' he advised her.

'What creek?' Hope asked, as she struggled to get herself up. 'Who are you?'

'Name's Jan Sprague, and it's lucky

for you I spotted the wagon. Them horses start moving again, it's likely to turn over,' he told her.

'Oh lawks!' said Hope, and let Sprague hand her down.

'Let me handle it,' he said. 'I'll get this wagon on to more even ground.'

Hope couldn't figure how on earth she had left the trail and gotten into such a predicament. Where was she? 'I guess I fell asleep,' she told the man, looking sheepish. She could see now that he was young, though probably older than she was. His blond hair hung on his collar, and he sported a drooping moustache. He was tallish and thin; had blue eyes which were giving her a good raking over. Hope was on her guard immediately.

'You all alone?' Sprague asked, after he'd moved the wagon well away from the creek. 'You sure got a parcel of horse flesh there. Where you heading?'

Hope ignored his questions and remark. 'Am I far from the trail?' she asked him.

'Not far. The horses probably smelled the water. It's not too safe for a woman on her own out here. If that's what you be,' he said enquiringly.

'I know, that's why I was travelling at night to get through Vernon. I heard it's a rough place,' Hope said, still giving the stranger no inkling as to why she was there or where she was going. Truth was, she still had no idea where she was headed.

'It sure is! Then most places out here in the West are rough,' Sprague replied. 'If you need help, then I could — well, them horses are sure a temptation to Indians, and trail-thieves. Hell, girl, ain't you got no sense? Had I been one o' them, you'd be dead now and everything taken,' he said exasperatedly.

Hope flushed. 'I wasn't alone until . . . well, it's a long story,' she closed up.

'None of my business, I reckon,' said Jan, making to get on to his horse. 'Like I told you. I'd be willing to help. I've got nothing better to do right now.'

Hope was thinking quickly. What had she to lose? He might follow her anyway. Better to know where he was at. 'All right! I'm going north-west to Denver. Right now I could use some coffee. How about you?'

A broad smile lit up Jan Sprague's face. 'I sure could, and some breakfast. I only got beans though,' he said, apologetically.

'Well I've got some deer meat,' said Hope.

'Let's get a fire built then. Be best over in the trees out of sight. We don't want no nosy company,' Sprague said, taking charge.

'That would be best,' said Hope. She got up and took the reins, clicking the horses on. Before she got down she slipped the sharp knife into her skirt pocket.

They ate the beans and meat, and some dried biscuits which Hope had found in a tin. They drank the coffee saying little, each wary of the other, a myriad of questions on their minds. The horses were browsing contentedly at the long grass within the trees. Hope began to relax. 'What are you doing out here?' she ventured. 'Do you live around here?'

'Nope, I'm travelling; was leastwise. I was looking for work, only this time of year the ranchers ain't hiring,' Sprague said, vaguely.

'So, you're a cowboy then?'

'Not really. I'm not overly fond of hazing cattle an' all that stuff. I can do it. Can do most kinds of hard labour, only the pay's no good.'

'Have you no family then?'

'Had once. I ran away when I was twelve. My pa drank, and there was seven of us.'

'Where did you live?'

'Oh, back in Kentucky. I've been to Mexico, Arizona, Colorado — lots of places. It's good being free. Look at all that space out there. You can ride for days an' not see anyone, only deer, coyotes and sometimes buffalo, only they're mostly gone north now. Used to be millions of 'em until they were slaughtered. Bones everywhere. My grandpa once told me, he saw 'em. It could take all day for a herd to pass, the noise like thunder, so he said,' Sprague laughed.

Seeing the look on Jan's face, Hope warmed to him. It was as if he visualized the whole scene. She felt a stirring of excitement take over her whole body. 'Listen,' she said. 'I want to sell the wagon and all but two of the horses. Do you know where I can do that and not get robbed?' she asked, flushing profusely.

Sprague studied her. 'Well, most horse dealers will try to do you down, especially as you're a woman. A rancher might buy the saddle mounts.'

'There's saddles too,' Hope interjected.

'Have you papers for all of the horses?'

'Oh Lord! I never thought — might have for the wagon and those two. I'll

61

have to look. The others, no!'

'That'll be tricky,' said Sprague, giving her a speculative look. 'It isn't easy without the bills of sale. Which ones are you planning to keep'

'The sorrel, and the copper one,' Hope said, positively.

'The roan looks good to me. The dun too. They all seem like good horses.'

'I don't want those two. The sooner they're gone the better. I can't handle the wagon — well, it's hard work. I could use the sorrel as a pack-horse, and ride the other. He's sort of special.'

'He's a deep bay. You brush him up he'll shine real nice. You sure they're not stolen,' Sprague said, regarding her closely.

Hope gave him a frozen look. 'I never stole them! Their owners — they're all dead. The owners of the wagon too. We were . . . ' Hope got up and walked off.

Sprague watched her go down to the

creek where she suddenly sat down. Her shoulders were heaving like she was bawling. Something bad must have happened on the trail to that girl, he thought. He took out the makings and shaped a cigarette. He did some figuring in his head. Lubbock and Amarillo were cowtowns. In both towns were saddlery shops. Might be they could get a good price for the saddles. If the owners of the horses were dead, then nobody would be looking for them. Still, she could be lying. It seemed strange. An idea came to him and Jan got up and walked down to join the girl. He could see she'd been crying, as she swung her face away. He sat down next to her. 'You got a name I can use?' he asked her softly.

'Bennett, Hope Bennett,' she responded.

Sprague laughed. 'Hope springs eternal!' He asked of her, 'Those folks that are dead. Were they your parents, relatives, maybe?'

'No, just friends. We were attacked at a water hole. They were killed.'

Hope sniffed, and took a handkerchief from her pocket.

'How come you got away then?' he asked.

'A man came just in time. He helped. He shot one of the robbers. We were going to Vernon, but the second one shot Sam, and then he forced me to drive away with him. He was vile. I killed him. I had to . . . ' Hope put her face into her hands and began to weep.

Sprague put an arm around her. 'You have a good cry. I reckon you've done real well on your own. An' you just a child, really!'

Hope looked up at him. 'I'm eighteen! I haven't been a child for years!' she said heatedly.

'Come on,' Sprague took her hand. 'We'd best get moving. Tomorrow, I'll take one horse and saddle, and try to sell 'em. Best that way. Tell me, what happens after you've got rid of everything and got to Denver? Why up there?' he asked, puzzled.

'My uncle lives there, only I haven't heard from him for over a year, nor seen him in three,' Hope replied. 'I don't really know if he's still there,' she added miserably.

'OK, then first things first, Hope Bennett. We'll take it one day at a time,' said Sprague, smiling at her reassuringly.

Hope smiled back at him. It was difficult not to respond to his exuberance. Perhaps she shouldn't have told him so much, but it had just come tumbling out. She felt a whole lot better as they walked back to the fire, and started to pack up.

# 5

Sam Carver had been in the mountains tracking two outlaws; both killers and robbers. He was cold, tired and in need of a hot bath. Bounty-hunting sure was a hard way to make a living. Perhaps he would quit after he got them both to Lubbock. He'd had to make a travois for the one he'd shot. Without evidence there would be no pay-out.

By the time Sam reached Fort Sumner he was exhausted. He left Otis in the fort's jailhouse, the horses and the stiff under a lean-to, and after some hot food he stretched out on a bunk where the army's guides slept.

Six days later Carver arrived in Lubbock as a blizzard swept across the plains, with one very stiff stiff, and Otis in poor condition.

'You'll get your dough in a week or so,' the sheriff told Sam, after locking

66

up Otis, and the money that Sam had retrieved off the robbers.

'You'd better not let that murderer escape,' said Sam.

'Hardly likely. They'd string me up if I did. Paul Kinross, the bank clerk, was a decent young man. I'll have my work cut out stopping a lynching. Was no need to have killed him,' McIvor said angrily.

'What's this?' Sam asked, holding up a poster showing a vague sketch of a young man with full beard.

'Ah! That's just come in. Apparently he's been after the stage coaches, and hitting on ranchers at their homes. Seems as if he watches from someplace, then slips in when there's hardly anybody about. He wears black mostly, and masks his face. He might have an accomplice. A posse chased him clear across the Pecos, and then lost him. He just vanished!'

'Has he killed anyone?'

'Not as is known. Could have in some other territory. Who knows? It does seem as if he's familiar with these parts,' McIvor opined.

'I can't do much until he appears again somewhere,' Sam said thoughtfully. 'Anyway, I'll be around awhile. I need a rest.' He left the jailhouse and went to put his horse away, then got a room at the hotel and slept for several hours.

★ ★ ★

Hope Bennett heard the whistle and sprang up off the couch. Through the window she saw Jan riding up at the edge of the timber.

Sprague sprang down as Hope opened the door. He handed her a gunny-sack, giving her a brief grin, then he took the roan horse around to the rear of the cabin where the other two horses greeted them noisily.

Hope gave Jan a studied look as he shrugged out of his sheepskin outer coat. She placed a mug of coffee on the hearth as he dropped into a buffalo

68

hidebound chair, a bottle of whiskey in his hand. He poured a liberal amount into the coffee. 'It sure is cold,' he said wearily.

'I wish we could go some place and get some land and settle,' Hope looked anxiously at him. 'I hate it when you go off for so long.'

'I told you. As soon as we have a nice pile of dough, we can go wherever we like. We'll have a real nice place like the rich folk. We deserve it. There's no job we can do that'd get us more than peanuts. I don't intend slaving to make others rich. We've been over it before,' Jan told her irritably. He poured more whiskey into the mug.

'I wish you wouldn't drink so much.'

Giving her a dark look, Jan said, 'I gotta have something to warm me, since you're so damned cold.'

Hope turned away and went to empty the sack of the provisions he had brought. It was now three months since Jan had brought her to this high plateau. First, he had managed to sell the wagon and team to a farmer in Amarillo, and then the two spare horses with saddles to a shifty sort of character at Fort Sumner. They had spent only two nights there, as the soldiers and other devious types had given Hope lascivious looks, the sort she was all too familiar with. Of course, she had been robbed over the sales, getting half of what they were worth. At least she had then had money of her own, something she had never had before. If Sam Carver hadn't been shot, there might have been what the Morrises and the other two had on them. She was sure it couldn't have been much. She had found a few dollars in a box in the wagon, and some letters to the Morrises from her uncle. After reading them she'd felt certain he hadn't really wanted her, as he'd indicated that Hope would have to work, probably for a rich family. That was why she had stuck with Jan.

He had been her only hope. Without him she would certainly have ended up — God knows where, and doing something quite unsavoury. What Jan did was wrong, but he was kind to her. She was under no illusions that he might, one day, just ride off and leave her. Once, after he'd been drinking, he had tried forcing himself on her. She had pulled out the knife and he'd let go of her, rather shaken. 'I'll kill you if I have to,' Hope had told him, in no uncertain terms. All she wanted was friendship, nothing more.

The hideaway, Hope knew, was safe enough. When Jan had led her right in under the waterfall, and along a narrow winding track so treacherous she had been terrified, and then up into the lush meadow which was surrounded by timber and high peaks, she had loved it.

He had never said how he'd found such a place, nor whose grave it was some yards from the cabin. Whoever had built the cabin had done a good job.

One reason Hope could not give herself to Jan Sprague was that she still thought often about Sam. She liked Jan well enough. His life had been not unlike her own. There was bitterness in him, though. He hated people who were those he described as plunderers. Rich, unfeeling bastards! She had much sympathy with his resentful outbursts and had pushed her misgivings out of her thoughts. The money he had stolen he kept secreted away somewhere in a tin box. He was generous enough with her. He had bought her a new riding outfit, and boots. She had bought toilet items and new underwear at the trading post near the fort. She had also acquired a warm winter coat, and a couple of winter shirts for Jan. Her own money was almost gone now. Jan had laughed at her sheer delight in being able to buy things for the first time. 'You'll be able to buy trunks of clothes soon, just like them ranchers' wives and daughters, and them Eastern folks,' he had promised.

After the months of hiding, often wondering if Jan had been caught — or worse, killed — her nerves were beginning to fray a little. Tracks were easy to find in the snow. One day he would be caught, she felt sure. He seemed unusually quiet, she thought, giving him a sideways glance.

'You seem in a bad mood,' Hope ventured, as she prepared some greens for the meal.

'I almost got caught two nights ago, near Tularosa. I think they were bounty-hunters,' Jan told her.

'What were you doing there?' Hope looked aghast.

'I went to buy whiskey. The saloon was full of rangemen and some real bad trail-hawks. I'd hit a coach on the northward trail; took nearly a thousand, got away clean, and figured it was OK to stop. I was on my way back and soon after I'd left town I made a stop. I heard horses coming, then bullets hit the trees. I was into the saddle and away fast. I guess they didn't have the night-eyes like me. I left 'em behind real fast,' Jan told her, then laughed.

'You didn't lead them to the river? They'll see your tracks,' Hope said worriedly.

'Nope! I circled, waited under a bank, and when it was near daylight I rode over to Bent. I played poker with a couple of prospectors.'

'They'll remember you, especially if a posse goes asking around. You're too careless, Jan,' Hope remonstrated frustratedly.

'We'll move out. We can't stay up here in the winter, we'd be blocked in. We have dough. We can go south and stay in a hotel someplace, and have us a good time. Later, we can go to Texas and try different counties. That's where the real money is. Cattle country! You can travel as my wife, it would be best. Don't worry, you can put a pillow between us,' Jan said, grinning. 'I can't think what the hell you're saving yourself for,' he said scathingly, and poured himself another large whiskey.

'Tomorrow we'll go. So you better start packing what you need.'

★ ★ ★

Sheriff McIvor sought out Carver, who was in Fred's Eating House, putting away a hefty breakfast. Finding him, he drew out a chair, sitting opposite Sam, and called over his shoulder for coffee.

'Morning, Don!' said Sam, looking up, wondering what the sheriff had on his mind.

A boy brought the coffee and set it down. 'Morning,' McIvor uttered. 'I sure do envy folks who have indoor jobs — this time of year.' He pulled a poster from a pocket. 'You might be interested in this,' he told Sam.

Carver smiled; McIvor rarely shifted himself from his office unless he was forced to. Sam looked at the fresh poster. It was almost the same as before but giving the latest places the outlaw had been seen in. 'I see he's been seen near Brownfield. Hit a coach. Some of the ranchers carry plenty of dough in their wallets.'

'Well, it's up to you,' McIvor said, and got up to leave. 'Could be a mite warmer to the south.'

'I see there's a thousand on him. I'll see what I can find out, I'll head for Brownfield,' Sam said, wiping his plate clean with a piece of bread.

An hour later Sam rode on out, leading a pack-horse with his gear on it. It sounded as if the robber was heading south. A few months ago, someone fitting the same description had been up around Amarillo. He was most likely heading south for the winter, and that'd suit him better, too, Sam thought.

★ ★ ★

Jan Sprague and Hope Bennett had covered a lot of miles since leaving their hideaway. Hope was tired and wiped away a stray tear. It was not as warm as she'd expected, down on the plains. Sweetwater was a miserable place. She found herself thinking of Vicksburg. Although her life there had been dreary, very boring and without hope, it had been more civilized. Nothing had prepared her for this western lifestyle, though she did often marvel at the things she saw, such as the flora and fauna, and the marvellous sunsets. The Great Dividing Range was quite awesome. If only she could persuade Jan to settle somewhere soon. He had enough to buy land.

Jan came in, closing the door noisily. After removing his outer garments, he poured himself a large whiskey into a less than clean glass. 'Ain't much of a place,' he said. 'It'll do for a few days.'

'Then where?' Hope asked disconsolately.

'It depends. I can say I'm looking for work. You just rest, and don't forget you're Mrs Sprague.'

'Surely you have enough money now.

Can't we get some land? I'm sick of travelling. If only I had my own money,' Hope said wistfully.

'Then you'd do what? You've got no talent. You couldn't even work in a whorehouse. Without me you would be lost,' Jan told her scathingly.

'Why don't you leave me then? Since I'm so useless to you!' She could read and write though, better than he could.

Sprague turned away. Damn it! If only she would be his wife in the true sense. 'All right! The next job I do you can help. Cut your hair short, wear pants, you could pass for a man. We make two or three good hauls, and split it. Then we can get us a real nice home,' he said convincingly.

Hope sat up. 'You mean it?' she asked excitedly.

'Sure,' said Jan. 'Why the hell not?'

★ ★ ★

Two days later, Sprague paid the bill, and he and Hope were on their way, going south. Later, they cut across to Abilene, arriving in the early evening. They went into a café which was full of drovers and locals. After they'd eaten, Jan walked the street noting the two banks, and the layout. He smelt money. Lots of it. He fetched Hope and they rode on out of town. When about three miles out, they turned off into a dry-wash and under some cottonwoods made camp. 'Tomorrow, I'll go back and check the main bank — see what kind of safe they have,' Jan told Hope.

'I don't think it wise,' said Hope. There's too many people about, and plenty of lawmen, I think.'

'Midday, that's the best time,' Jan ignored her anxious plea. 'You can be across the street with the horses. Folks will be heading on home to eat.'

'You're mad!' said Hope. 'The manager and clerks, they'll have guns. You'll be shot!'

'They'll be tied up. A simple plan. It will work, and we'll be long gone before anyone finds 'em.'

'They'll see your face. They will hunt you down.'

'I'll put my hat down, wear my bandanna. There'll be plenty of dough in that bank,' Jan said, grinning.

★ ★ ★

The young bank clerk strode across the floor to close the door. 'We're closing,' he told the man with his back to him, after ushering the last customer out.

Sprague, who was fumbling with his bandanna, suddenly pulled his Colt and got behind the clerk. 'Lock it and be quick,' he spoke into Earl Tucker's ear.

His hand trembling, Earl locked the door. Sprague took the key, and put it in his own pocket.

A voice came from the doorway to the rear. 'Earl, you locked up yet?'

'Answer him,' Sprague pushed his Colt at Tucker's back, as he moved him forward.

'Yes, Mr Greene,' he croaked.

The manager came forward, looking impatient. His mouth fell open, and he gulped.

'Down on the floor,' Sprague ordered the portly man who wore steel-framed glasses. When Jan got close to him he whipped them off, as Greene lowered himself awkwardly to the floor. Jan put a foot on his neck.

Tucker was putting money from two drawers into a bag that Jan had given him. 'That's all!' he told Sprague when the drawers were empty.

'The safe, there must be more in there. Fill another bag, be quick,' he ordered Tucker.

'It's locked,' Tucker spluttered.

'Listen, you. Get it open. There must be a key.'

'Mr Greene has it,' said Tucker feebly.

'Then get it off him,' Sprague snarled, shoving the clerk hard in the ribs.

After Tucker had retrieved the key

from Greene, he unlocked the safe and gathered some wads of notes off a shelf. Sprague was beginning to sweat, time was moving on. 'That will do,' he called. 'Put it into that saddle-bag on the counter.'

While Tucker locked the safe again, Sprague took some rawhide thongs from a pocket. 'Tie him up,' he motioned to the manager, and bent and put some cloth into the quivering man's mouth.

Tucker was shaking badly, and with difficulty he got Greene's wrists tied. Then Sprague told him to get down, and very quickly he tied the clerk's wrists and ankles, then he gave him a rap over the head with the Colt, and left him sprawled over Greene's body. He was at the door quickly, and unlocking it he passed through, then locked it again and threw the key under the boardwalk. He went quickly across the street, the saddle-bags over his arm.

Hope had brought the horses up a

side street five minutes ago. She was fussing with the cinch of the sorrel as two riders went down the hard-rutted street. They took little notice of her as they headed for the saloon. It was quiet now, most folks had gone to partake of their midday meals. It was very cold and not a day to be outdoors unless one had to be.

Sprague put the saddle-bags over the horn, mounted and set off eastwards. 'Let's go,' he said quietly to Hope. When they were well down the trail, they went into a steady lope. About twenty minutes later they went into the wash where they picked up the pack-horse, Sam Carver's Mike, and headed across country. By the time it was dark they had found a sheltered place where they made camp.

First, they made a low fire and heated coffee, then sat trying to relax. After they were more or less in a calmer frame of mind, they counted the money.

'Sixty thousand!' Hope gasped. 'It's

a fortune! I never thought you could do it. I was really scared.'

Grinning widely, Sprague got up, grabbed her and executed a jig with her along the hollow. 'We can go anywhere we please now. I told you, didn't I? One or two more like this, and we'll be rich,' he said, his eyes alight.

'We'll have to lie low now,' said Hope, sobering. 'Did they see your face?'

'No! I wore a bandanna. They never even noticed me until they were locking up.'

'Somebody will remember us. I'm sure. There'll be a posse out, you can count on that!'

'They don't know which way we went. They don't know there was two of us. We'll move on south. In about ten days we could be into San Antonio, then we'll have us a good time. I'll have to get some of this dough into a bank, I can't carry so much around. It'd be hard to explain if some nosy sheriff was to find it, should I get caught,' Jan said wisely.

Hope lay back under her blanket, her mind in a whirl. Even though she'd been scared, it had been exciting. The exhilaration had worn off now, and her thoughts dwelt on more sensible things. This was no kind of life. If they kept on, they would surely be caught one day.

'Jeez, it's cold,' Jan said. He got up and put more wood on the fire, then he came and got under the blanket beside her, drawing his own over them.

Hope said nothing. Jan was right. One had to look after oneself; nobody else would. Soon they slept.

# 6

When he came to Brownfield, Sam Carver discovered little about the stage-coach robber. He felt very undecided as to whether he should still ride south or go after other outlaws whom he had picked up warranties on. It might well be most of them had gone south for the winter. Perhaps he should be satisfied with the amount of money he had lodged in a bank at Fort Worth, and buy some land. This wanderlust he had in him was a nuisance. He was still undecided, standing by his horses, when a voice hailed him. 'Hey, Carver!' A deputy came up to him. 'We've just had a telegraph. A bank's been robbed at Abilene. A lot of dough taken, and it says one fella done it. Cool as yer please jest at closing time. Took what he wanted, locked the door and rid off.'

'Any description?' Sam asked.

'Youngish. Had his face covered, but he had a beard. Sounds like that loner. There's a thousand posted on him. He could've gone anywhere, though!'

'Well, I might as well go find out what I can,' Sam told the deputy, and got mounted. He rode eastwards, feeling the edge of a raw wind.

* * *

Jan and Hope rode steadily southward, stopping only for meals at small settlements they came upon. Many of the people they met were Mexican. One or two of the men eyed Hope with lusting looks which made her shiver. On the fourth day they decided to rest the horses a day or two. They found a place where they were well hidden, and not far from a creek. Hope managed to wash their dirty clothing and hung it on some bushes to dry out in the sun, which had more warmth in it now, she noticed. She sat enjoying the respite, her nerves calmed. She was beginning to take delight in this semi-desertland. Never before had she been so aware of nature. Jan warned her about the creatures she must look out for, such as scorpions, snakes and the prickly bushes. She turned to him, and tried once again to encourage him to buy land and settle somewhere.

'Sure, that's what we'll do. I've told you so. We need more dough so we won't ever want for nothing. If you make up your mind to marry me,' he said, giving her a hungry look.

Hope shrugged. 'I won't marry an outlaw. I couldn't stand the worry,' she told him.

'Right!' Jan got up. He went to the saddle-bags and took out some notes. 'Here, take it. There's twenty thousand. You can find yourself a little house. You could get a job — do whatever you want. Go look for your uncle. You've gotta decide now,' he told her in strident tone.

Hope pushed the money away. 'You

got it. I didn't do anything except tag along. When we get to San Antonio I'll find work. Perhaps in a café or something. I still have a few dollars left,' she said tearfully.

Jan walked off. 'Stubborn as hell she is,' he muttered. She wouldn't last a week without me. Some bastard would get his hands on her. Truth was, she had gotten under his skin. She showed no signs that there'd ever be more than an uneasy friendship between them. What the hell did she want?

When they passed through Fredericksburg where many Germans had settled, Jan was sure this was a place where he could realize his dreams. It was ranchland. He could buy books on ranching in San Antonio, look around the country. He became on fire with ambition. Yes, he would need a lot of dough, then he could be one of the wealthy lot. Somehow, he would persuade Hope to stick with him. He would need a wife.

After, they had stabled the horses in

a small livery not far from a hotel, which Jan noted was in a side street. Not like the big fancy one they had ridden past but one where they would not be out of place.

'We need two rooms, adjoining,' he told the clerk at the small counter. 'My wife would like a hot bath prepared, soon as possible. If you can't accommodate us, then we'll have to go elsewhere,' Jan said, emulating one of the smart easterners he had once heard in Denver.

The clerk spluttered. 'It will take a while, but we can oblige, sir.' He took the five dollars Jan gave him and swung the register round.

'We'll be staying a while,' said Jan. 'You look after us, OK?' He signed in as Mr and Mrs J. Sprague, Tulsa, Oklahoma. He turned and winked at Hope.

Swallowing hard, the clerk handed Jan two keys for the only adjoining rooms the hotel had. He watched the two rather shabby young folks go upstairs, wondering why they wanted two rooms. A moment later he dashed off to the kitchen to order the hot bath.

After they had eaten their evening meal in the rather small dining-room, and Jan had escorted Hope back up to her room, he told her to keep the doors locked. He would be out for a while looking over the town.

Once out on the street, Jan walked to the main one and stood some moments. The lighting was poor when he turned off into another street on hearing piano music. He saw a saloon and above the batwings the name Blue Bonnet. He also noted, further along the street, men coming out of a large three-storeyed building, and he went to investigate. He had not guessed wrong, as Jan saw when he entered. A strong aroma of tobacco smoke and heavy perfume attacked his nostrils, as a thin-lipped, black-haired, tall, middle-aged woman came forward. She raked her eyes over Sprague, knowing immediately which of her girls to offer the bearded young man with the long shaggy hair. She called to a heavy-set man hovering near her office. 'Jack, go call Dolores,' she told him, in a crisp, no-nonsense tone. 'It'll be ten dollars,' she told Sprague. 'Do you wish a bottle of anything?'

'Nothing, thank you,' Jan said, producing the money. Without another word, he followed the young Mexican girl up a staircase and into a spartan, ill-lit room.

Half an hour later, Sprague sat at a large round table in a corner of the saloon bar, at the Blue Bonnet. He felt relaxed after his call at the whore-house. He had also felt lucky. Just before midnight, he pulled out of the poker game $2,000 richer. Before he reached his hotel, however, he was suddenly set upon by two or three men he felt sure were Mexicans. He had seen them sitting at a table, while playing poker. They hit him hard, and kicked him, until he lost consciousness. It was some time before he came round from a last blow on the head. By the time he got himself back to his room the night was well on.

When Hope, next morning, on going through to his room, saw the fury in Jan's eyes, her heart began to thump. She had seen that look once before and it really frightened her. 'Lord! What happened to you?' she asked as he tried to sit up, and she saw the bruises.

Jan told her about the poker game, and how he had won. 'I was on my way back, just after midnight.'

'Well, I'm surprised at you getting caught like that, you're usually more careful,' she said, somewhat casually. It had occurred to her that, should Jan one day have a great deal of money, he might well take up bad ways and go through it very quickly. 'I think you should stay in bed. You might have concussion. If I were you, I'd go put your money into a bank where it will be safe. You could easily have it taken off you along the trail. All these Mexicans about and God knows who else. I'll have some food sent up to you.' Hope swept out of the room leaving Jan in thoughtful mood. She sure was a cool one.

★ ★ ★

After speaking with the sheriff in Abilene, and a couple of rangehands, who said they'd seen someone holding two horses, one a roan, the other a deep bay, on the day of the robbery, Sam Carver had a nasty gut feeling he didn't like. His horse, Mike, could easily fit the bay's description, and the roan the one Lew had owned. Sam wished heartily that he could catch up with them. Nobody had noticed which way they had gone, unfortunately. It did seem, though, that he or they, were moving south. He decided to go as far as San Antonio, a place he had never been to. It did not matter really where he went. At each place he came to he made enquiries. On the third day he came upon a Mexican who said he worked for a rancher. He also told Sam that he had seen two riders come out of a dry-gulch, riding the horses Sam had described to him, and leading a sorrel pack-horse. The *vaquero* figured they must have spent the night there.

'Did you see what they looked like?' Sam asked, his mind in a whirl.

'Not big. I not up close. They ride south, *señor*.

'*Muchas gracias*,' said Sam, and rode away beginning to sweat. It sure as hell sounded as if he was on the right trail. Could it be coincidence, a roan, a bay and a sorrel? Who were they? Was it Lew? He had been in his thirties, heavy-set and not small. Then he would not look big or small from a distance.

A week later at Fredericksburg, Sam heard again of the riders who had stopped at a store. One had longish light-coloured hair and a lot of beard. The other had stayed with the horses and seemed young. 'Might be a younger brother,' the old timer told Sam. 'The horses were good stock.'

'How long ago?' asked Sam anxiously.

'Week or more. Cain't rightly say. Was kinda cold an' the saloon window was a mite steamed up. They was riding off when I went outside. Southwards, I reckon they was headed.'

If they were the robbers, Sam speculated, they might be headed for San Antonio. The banks there would have plenty of dough. On the other hand, being as they'd got such a pile at Abilene they could hole up and enjoy themselves and then move on somewhere else. Figuring they would need to rest sometime, Sam plodded on. Perhaps those two were heading for Mexico; Laredo was a favourite spot for bandits, they could slip across the Rio Grande and disappear. They seemed young though to be on the outlaw trail. Perhaps that's why nobody suspects them, Sam thought.

★ ★ ★

After Jan Sprague had rested for two days, he got up and went to the National Bank. He deposited $5,000. 'I would like to open an account in Austin, also,' he told the manager. 'If you would deposit $2,000 there for me, I'd be obliged. My wife and I have just arrived from Galveston, and are looking around for a home. We aren't sure where it will be. I don't like carrying money around on me, there are so many outlaws about, so I've heard.'

The manager took the $7,000, smiling ingratiatingly. 'Of course, Mr Sprague, we are glad to be of service.'

The next day Jan bought a ticket on the stage-coach for Austin and deposited the rest of his money into three different accounts in different banks. When he got back and told Hope, though he didn't mention how he had spread it around, she felt somewhat placated. During his absence she had enjoyed herself looking at the shops, especially the big Emporium.

She had seen some of the wealthy ranchers' wives buying up new dresses that had been shipped down from back East. It had fired her imagination when Jan told her. 'You stick with me, we'll have the best, just like them folks. Tonight we'll put on our best clothes, after I've been and got rid of this beard and taken a good soak. I got a real nice suit in Austin. We'll go have a fine meal in that Alamo Restaurant.' Hope's eyes lit up, and catching his enthusiasm, she took out the new dress she had bought.

The meal was the best they had ever had. Fresh trout with potatoes and green vegetables, and imported wine which made Hope giggly. They also had a fluffy dessert with fresh cream, and large brandies, Jan showing off with a Havana cigar. The waiter was delighted with the tip Jan gave him, and said he hoped they would come again. By the time they got back to the hotel in one of the smart carriages for hire, Hope was ecstatic. Jan was right, she would stick with him. Never had she enjoyed herself so, or even dreamed how life could be. Yes, it took money, but they would have it. Plenty!

As Jan helped undress Hope she was hardly aware of where she was, or what she was doing, and certainly not of his intentions. Quickly he got her into bed then cast off his own clothing, and was in beside her, covering her with warm kisses.

When it was over, Sprague lay with an arm under her as Hope slept soundly. A satisfied smile spread across his face. Now perhaps she would realize how good it could be if she would only be his wife. After he had slept awhile he got up. He took his good suit into his room and hung it in the wardrobe and taking out his western gear, got dressed and tied on his holster belt. Before he left the room he wrote out a brief note for Hope to say he'd be gone a few days. He left some dollars in her carpet-bag, picked up his rifle and left. He went out through the kitchen where it was too early for anyone to have arrived yet. He then collected the roan from the livery stable and was soon riding southwards, whistling softly to himself. When he was off alone like this, Jan felt alive; so free. There was something about this vast land that gripped him with excitement. It was something he couldn't explain, even to himself.

# 7

When Hope awoke she had an awful taste in her mouth. A shaft of sunlight came in between the gap in the curtains. She sat up groaning at the pain in her head. Feeling her nakedness, the significance of last evening hit her. She exploded, 'Damn him! He got me drunk!'

Irritated with herself, Hope got out of bed and, pouring cold water from a jug into the washbasin, she washed herself all over, then vigorously rubbed her body dry. As she was slipping into her skirt she saw a piece of paper propped against the lamp. Snatching it up she read the poor scrawl. My Lord, Jan had better learn to write and spell if he wanted to elevate himself, she thought critically. The note simply told her he'd be gone for a few days, and he had left money in her carpetbag.

Hope sat down. 'Damn him!' she said again. What would folks think as she took her meals all alone? She sniffed into her handkerchief. Well, maybe she'd be gone when he got back. Down in the dining-room she refused breakfast, taking only coffee, then left in a hurry. Back up in her room a thought struck her. What if Jan had ridden off and left her? She went to his wardrobe and checked — his two suits hung on a rail and his spare clothes were still in a drawer. His saddle-bags and guns were gone. Searching in her purse in the carpetbag she found $300. That was something, and she still had a few dollars of her own.

Putting on her warm wool coat and strong shoes, Hope went down, passing the gaping clerk whose lusting thoughts ran rampant whenever he saw her. There were few pedestrians on the sidewalk, the day being very chill, but a bright sun hit her in the eyes as she headed straight for the Emporium. Her mind was set on buying herself a watch, something she had always wanted. She pulled her velour hat down to shield her face and therefore did not see the tall man riding down the opposite side of the street, leading a pack-horse. Sam Carver did not recognize the young woman leaning against the wind as she turned a corner. He truly believed Hope Bennett was either dead and buried in some remote lonely grave or long gone from these parts. Her good looks and pretty hair, however, often came to mind as he plodded his lonesome trails.

Reining in at a café, Sam tied his horses at the hitching-rack and took his saddle-bags and rifle in with him. In the past few days he'd seen plenty of Mexicans and, in his experience, there were those amongst them who'd slit your throat without hesitation, and steal your gear quicker than greased lightning. He'd lost his horse, Mike, and a good rifle because of his carelessness only six months ago. He was on his guard. He found a table by the window from where he could see the street. Watching folks, you could learn a lot about a town, Sam reckoned. A young girl came to take his order. 'Meat and potatoes, miss,' he told her. 'None of that chilli stuff, it don't suit my innards.'

* * *

Jan Sprague shivered as he stood in the shadows. He had looked in over the half-door and seen the greaser hovering at the far end of a rough bar. The barman at the Blue Bonnet Saloon, after Jan had given him five dollars, had told Jan who he thought was responsible for beating him and taking his winnings. Henderson had noticed how the three Mexicans had left the saloon only moments after Jan. They might work on one of the ranches, he'd said.

The cantina was not well lit, was full of tobacco smoke and stank of body-sweat and chilli peppers. The room was full of *vaqueros*, local squatters, and some devious characters who'd stopped off for refreshment. Jan was certain now that the man at the bar had been in the Blue Bonnet. Two men seated at a table, with girls on their laps, were laughing and talking loudly. He believed they had also been there that night. He went round to the rear of the cantina and put a hand to the three horses tethered there. They were still warm, their legs splattered with mud, as if they'd been ridden some distance. It was no secret that the Texas Rangers were hard stretched, and lawmen frequently got shot. No sheriff would bother chasing bandits who just slipped down to the border, crossed the Rio Grande and disappeared. Henderson had told Jan he should get a money-belt, and take care after leaving the card tables.

No damn greaser was getting away with his dough. That $2,000 he had come by honestly. He could, of course, do as they had done, but it didn't appeal to him, and he wasn't a violent person. He had never killed anyone, only defended himself when he had to. His father had once told him, Don't never let anyone put you down, son. Do unto them as they do to you. Jan smiled thinly. As far as he recalled, his father had slept in a lot of ditches, too drunk to get up. He'd probably drunk himself to death by now, he thought sadly. Quickly, he slipped the reins of the three horses from the rack and, running between some adobes, he went out into the plain. The ground was crisp, the moon bright. When he came to the cottonwoods where he'd left his roan, the horses nickered loudly. He tied them to a branch, mounted Nippy, the name he'd given the roan since he had a tendency to turn and nip at one, if he could get away with it, and rode back in between the adobes, dismounted and stood leaning against the horse. It was gone midnight and all the dwellings were in darkness.

Two *vaqueros* were the first to leave.

They mounted their horses at the front of the cantina and were soon gone, the soft thudding of hoofs whispering away into the cold night. A few moments later two or three *putas* went noisily across the street and entered a large shack.

Sprague tensed as the two Mexicans with their *putas* came out. The girls were supporting them as they staggered across the street. They'd be staying the night, Jan figured. Where was the other one? A voice spoke in the doorway. '*Buenas noches, Juan! Hasta luego*!'

Another voice answered, '*Buenas noches, Carlos*!'

Jan heard the door slam shut and a dark shape appeared around the corner and came to a halt. '*Donde estan los caballos*?' the man said, in alarm.

Jan stepped forward, swinging the lariat he'd learned well how to use. Carlos Ferrer swung round, reaching for his pistol, but he was too late. The rope dropped over him, pinning his arms to his sides, and he dropped the pistol. He was jerked off his feet, and Jan got to him. He kicked the pistol away, then pulled some rawhide from his pocket, tied first the wrists, and then the ankles of the Mexican.

Ferrer swore vividly at Jan, as he pulled him up and got him to the roan. He lifted him up and flung him across the saddle, then got up behind him. When he had ridden about a mile away from the adobes, Jan got down and yanked the Mexican off the saddle, threw him on the ground and straddled him. 'Now, you thieving bastard! Where is the *dinero* you took from me when I came out of the Blue Bonnet Saloon?' he asked angrily.

Ferrer feigned surprise. '*Señor*, I do not know what you speak of. I have but few dollars.'

'Yeah, I'll bet!' Jan said. He eased himself up and loosened the rope so that he could go through the Mexican's pockets. He removed a knife he found up a sleeve. He saw a thong at his neck and yanked out the leather pouch, and withdrew some folded notes. There was less than a hundred dollars. 'Where's the rest?' Jan snarled, and gave Ferrer a punch in the ribs.

'I tell you *nada*, gringo!' Ferrer snarled, and spat at Sprague.

Sprague hit him again. 'You'd better tell me if you don't want to die,' Jan threatened him.

Ferrer played for time, though he was now quite afraid. 'I never see you before,' he lied.

'You're lying. The *dinero*, have you spent it?' Jan put the knife to Ferrer's throat, a trickle of blood ran down his neck.

'It was the young gringo at the poker table. He no like lose. He no like you win. He say we get back he give fifty dollars. He do this many times, *señor*.'

'You mean when he loses you get the *dinero* back. Who the hell is he?' Jan asked, perplexed.

'He Nick Kreutz. His papa, he is the big ranchero. Nick play *mucho* poker. He bad *hombre*,' Ferrer said, quaking.

'So, this Nick gives you the tip-off when he loses. You follow the one who has won the most, beat him up, take the *dinero* and give it to Kreutz. For this he gives all of you fifty dollars? Why in hell don't you keep the money yourselves?'

'We *vaqueros* at the rancho. He say he send back to Mexico, if we do not. He plenty bad, *señor*. He say you cheat!'

Jan got up. He untied the Mexican, but he kept his knife and the dollars. 'Listen, you thieving greaser. This time I let you go. I know it was you who hit me first. If I see you in San Antonio again, I'll have the sheriff lock you up. You *comprende*?'

Ferrer, looking furious, picked up his sombrero and slapped it against his leg before placing it back on his head, muttering in Mexican dialect.

'You better start walking,' Sprague told him, pulling his Colt, drawing back the hammer.

Ferrer turned to go. 'Hey, *vaquero*!' Jan called to him. 'Where is the rancho? What is it called?'

'The Lazy K, gringo!' Ferrer called over his shoulder. He walked away into the night, cold sweat inside his shirt. He hastened his step when he was some yards away. The bullet he expected did not come. One day, gringo! I'll get you. I not forget, he told himself angrily.

Sprague mounted Nippy and headed northwards up the trail. By the time it was growing light, he could see smoke spirals and buildings up ahead. A half hour later he sat in a café ravenously tucking into a good breakfast. His thoughts were on Hope. How would she greet him on his return? He told himself that what he did was all for her. One day they would own a fine big home, and folks would look up to them. Somehow he must get her to understand how he felt about her.

# 8

The more Sprague thought about Nick Kreutz, the more angry he became. The Mexican had said that Kreutz had helped beat him up. He couldn't let that go. As he rode up a trail he saw many cattle grazing, and when he saw some posts with a sign hanging between them that had The Lazy K Ranch on it, with F. R. Kreutz under it, Jan stopped and took in the endless miles of terrain. He urged Nippy on as an idea began to form in his mind, and a hardness spread over his face.

Best I go see Hope first, he figured. She'll be hopping mad. Might even have taken off. She'd not leave without her dough. He'd seen the glow in her eyes when he'd handed it to her. Took a lot of guts to hand it back. Hope was a determined person, there was no telling what she might do. He went into a lope.

It was almost dark when Jan put Nippy away. The ostler asked him how much longer he'd be staying.

'I can't say,' Jan told him, paid what he owed, and went to the hotel.

When he got into his room, Hope came through looking furious. 'So, you came back then?' she said cuttingly.

Throwing his saddle-bags on to a chair, he looked at her a moment. 'I thought about leaving but I got to thinking. Why don't we get married proper? What if you have a child? I reckon we get on OK. As good as folks do. You go it on your own you'd be lonely, and I'd miss you. Then if you was to take that dough I offered you, and let it out you wasn't poor, you'd soon find a husband; one you fancied,' Jan said, in scathing tone.

'You bastard — you took advantage of me! You got me drunk! You took the money back quick enough, you're an Indian giver,' Hope flung at him.

'Well, you'd only have gone off

spending it, and drawing folks' attention to us. We gotta be careful. I left you enough. Anyway, I've got an idea — we might be moving on soon. Only, if you won't marry me I'm going it alone. I got feelings! It ain't bad around here, we could get our own place. You'd better make up your mind,' Jan told her in no uncertain tone. He then took off his gunbelt, his boots, and dropped on to the bed.

Hope, shaken, saw the weariness in his face and a sort of desperation. She softened. He had looked well after her. God knows what would have happened to her if he hadn't found her that day by the creek . . . What had she to lose? What if she were with child? 'I'll think about it, Jan,' she said quietly. 'Shall I go bring some food up for you? You look real tired.'

'Sure, that'd be nice,' said Jan, and smiled at her.

★ ★ ★

114

The house Jan and Hope bought for peanuts was situated some six miles from town, not far from the river in amongst some trees, and there was a small creek, berry bushes and about three acres that had been cleared for growing whatever they wanted. All told, there were twenty acres. The house was two storeyed, with three bedrooms, a large kitchen, and living-room with a dining area at one end. Hope fell in love with it at once when she saw the big stone fireplace. It was well concealed and about half a mile off the trail. The house was in need of repair and had been left empty for more than a year since the previous owner, a wagon-train master who'd been shot in the back one night on his way home from town (which the land agent did not impart to the Spragues), had not left a will, and after many enquiries no relative had been found.

When Hope had finally said she would marry Jan, they had slipped up to Austin, found a preacher and a couple of witnesses, and made it official. Hope had made it clear to Jan that she was not going to be a slave to his needs. He had grinned, knowing how strong of mind she could be. They had spent two days at a good hotel, spent some money on new clothes, then come back and taken up residence in their first ever home of their own. Jan had hired a Mexican couple and had helped to put up a shack for them to live in, then set to repairing some outbuildings for stabling and for a couple of cows and some chickens he had bought. He had told Jaime and Alfreda Torres that he was a mining engineer, and sometimes he would be away prospecting. 'Then you will take care of the *señora* for me.' They had agreed gladly, only too happy to have a home, a small income and a *patron* who treated them well.

After a couple of weeks' hard grafting on the house, Jan told Hope he was going into town, perhaps to play some poker. 'I need some relaxation,' he said.

'For God's sake, be careful,' Hope told him. 'You know what happened the last time. Don't go to that saloon,' she said worriedly.

'I'll be OK,' Jan grinned at her. 'Lock the doors and keep the shotgun handy. The Torreses' dog will bark if anyone comes around. Jaime's cousin is visiting so you'll be all right.'

It was Saturday and the Blue Bonnet Saloon was very busy, Jan could see as he made his way to the bar. Henderson nodded. 'A beer,' Jan called to him as he turned to survey the room. His eyes took in the six men who sat at the far corner table playing poker. Nick Kreutz was one of them. Why he came to this saloon when there were others which folks of his stature patronized, he couldn't guess. Perhaps because he was a better player than the questionable characters who used the Blue Bonnet, and he could usually win. The men who were with him, though, seemed well dressed.

Jan's gaze shifted to another table

where four Mexicans were seated and were talking quietly and drinking their beer. *Vaqueros*, just like those who'd beaten and robbed him. That was the answer. Kreutz brought his associates here for a bit of local colour most likely, and if he was a loser he made sure he got his money back.

'You not playing tonight?' Henderson asked, as he came along the bar.

'The table is full,' Jan said, off-handedly. 'Those men with Kreutz, who are they?'

'They're cattlemen!' Henderson responded.

'Why here? Why not in the Long View or the Broken Wheel?' Jan queried.

Henderson shrugged. 'I guess Nick thinks they like a change. An' I guess they won't notice him dealing off the bottom so good.'

Jan smiled. He finished his beer and went out into the cold night air. He found a café still open, went inside and asked for coffee and pie. He might have a long wait for Kreutz. He took a folded newspaper from his sheepskin coat pocket and started to read. He was not good at reading, but he had plenty of time. Hope had told him he should improve his writing and spelling if he wanted to be somebody. She was learning the Mex lingo now, with Alfreda Torres. He sure was glad Hope had stuck with him.

Around midnight Jan left the café, which was closing. He walked back to the Blue Bonnet and stood looking over the batwings. It was almost empty now, but the poker players were still there. Two Mexicans still sat at a table, and three nondescript types looking as if they were drunk sagged in their seats next to a piano which was closed. An array of empty glasses littered their table. A bartender went over and cleared the debris away. 'You fellas better be on your way, it's closing time,' he said.

One of the men tried to get up, fell back again, giggling. 'Shit!' he said.

His two companions actually managed to rise. 'Come on, Joe,' one of them said, and hoisted him out of his chair. All three staggered to the batwings, managed to manoeuvre themselves out to the boardwalk where they swayed then fell over and lay in a heap, cursing and giggling.

A sound of chairs scraping drew Jan's attention and he saw that the poker game was breaking up. 'I guess you had the luck tonight, Kreutz!' he heard someone say.

'You win some, you lose some,' Kreutz responded cheerfully, putting away his winnings.

Moving quickly, Jan went to the main street where he had tied the sorrel. He'd decided to give Nippy a rest for a change. He loped out of town taking a south-west trail. Already, he had selected the spot where he would wait for Kreutz. He now knew the area well, having spent some time riding around after buying the house.

The night was crisp and cold, the

moon waning. He came to a stand of trees just off the trail in a hollow and swung down. He took his rifle out and jacked a shell into the breech and stood waiting. It suddenly occurred to him that Kreutz might not be alone. He wanted no gun play. He might have to let him go this time, he thought irritably. He stamped his feet to keep warm.

It was some twenty minutes or more before he heard a horse coming, and as it got closer, saw the vapour coming from its nostrils. There was just one rider and the horse was a buckskin. He pulled the bandanna up and stepped on to the trail. '*Hola!*' he called out. '*Alto, amigo!*'

Kreutz yanked on the reins and the horse slithered to a stop only inches from Sprague, who stood fast.

'What the hell!' Kreutz ejaculated. He'd been half asleep, having consumed a fair amount of whiskey. His hand slid to his sidegun, but it was under his thick coat.

Sprague moved fast, took hold of the right rein and shoved his rifle barrel up at Kreutz's chest. '*Señor*, toss your *cartera, por favor*. Don' make no move or I pull the trigger, *comprende*?'

'*Si, comprende*,' said Kreutz, wondering if he put his heels into the horse . . . The greaser had a tight hold on the rein, he daren't risk it. 'I don't have *dinero*. I lost it all at poker,' he said, playing for time, and getting very angry.

'You got *mucho*, you damned *cucaracha* — you give *pronto*.'

Kreutz was seething, and made a grab for the gun barrel. Jan dropped the rein, grabbed his arm and yanked Kreutz right out of the saddle. In a second he'd put down the rifle and taken a knife from his sleeve. Kreutz was face down and he straddled him, putting the knife at the side of his face. 'Don' move, *señor*, or you have the leetle accident,' Sprague told him, and gave him a tiny nick under the left ear. His hand slid inside the thick jacket and found the wallet in an inner pocket. Pulling it out he felt a thick wad of notes, grinned, and put it into his own pocket. He then took Kreutz's sidegun and tossed it down into the hollow. He put away the knife and yanked Kreutz up to his feet. He hit him hard in the ribs, then across the jaw. 'You go, gringo. You walk ver' quick. The *caballo*, he go home, I theenk,' Sprague said, then laughed in the back of his throat. He picked up the rifle, and gave the buckskin a hard whack over its rump, and it ran off down the trail in a hurry. 'Go, run!' he shouted at Kreutz.

Kreutz was almost sobbing with rage. Blood poured from his mouth, and his ribs hurt like hell. He walked off down the trail, hoping his horse would have stopped somewhere. He was damned if he was going to run, especially for a damned Spik. Somehow he would find out who the sonofabitch was, then he would kill him.

Jan went down into the hollow and

took off the poncho he had slipped over his coat while riding along the trail. He replaced the sombrero with his round-crowned hat, stuffed the items into a saddle-bag and swung up into the saddle. Before he set off he took a long swallow from the half-bottle of whiskey he had bought from Henderson. He rode out into the plain, and although he was only about four miles from home, he spent an hour riding where he knew the *vaqueros* had ridden to tend the cattle. Once or twice he back-tracked, then crossed the river. It was almost dawn when he hit the main trail, and loped on home. If Kreutz should try to find his tracks, he'd have one hell of a job, Jan reckoned, as he put the horse away. He gave him a rub down, and then went across to the house. The fire was gone down so he got it going again. It was only after he had made coffee, laced it with brandy, that he sat down and opened the wallet. 'Oh, wow!' he said when he had counted the notes. There was $11,000 in hundreds.

'Well, Kreutz, you sure ain't agoing to be feeling such a smart-ass now,' Jan laughed heartily.

When Jan slid in beside Hope, she said, sleepily, 'You have a good game? Did you win?'

'You could say that, hon,' he told her. 'Might be I'll buy you a present — a bonnet. A blue bonnet,' he said, chuckling, and drew her in to him.

'That'll be nice,' said Hope unenthusiastically.

# 9

Sam Carver, after due consideration, had decided that bounty-hunting was no longer a viable proposition. Of late, he'd had to draw on his savings to support himself. There were just too many chasing the same outlaws, some of them ready to put a bullet into your back and steal your captives. San Antonio was as good as any place to set down roots. He'd seen a few pieces of land in the area that he wouldn't mind having. He rode on down to the sheriff's office to see if any new warrants had come in. When he went inside he found sheriff Haywood talking with a captain of the Texas Rangers who was complaining bitterly about the vast territory he had to cover. 'I just don't have enough men,' he was telling Haywood.

'Hey, Sam!' Haywood hailed him.

'You ever thought of joining the Texas Rangers? This is Buck Adams. Captain Adams, to give him his correct title.'

Sam shook hands with Adams, and took a seat. Haywood passed him a mug of coffee. 'Might be the Rangers don't want an ex-bounty-hunter. I am familiar with a fair bit of the territory north and west of San Antonio, and some of the hang-outs of these outlaws.'

Buck Adams gave Carver a studied look. 'I just lost a good man and I need to replace him quick. If you're willing, I can take you on a three-month trial. You'll need a good horse,' he told Sam.

'I've got two,' said Sam. 'I can start tomorrow,' he told Adams, quickly making up his mind. A regular wage packet would be real nice for a change. It would give him time to save more dough, and also get a look around the county. He might even find himself a wife, he supposed, his thoughts running way out of control. Where the hell was Hope Bennett?

Adams got up. 'Shall we go discuss things over a bite to eat?' he asked Sam.

'Surely,' Sam said eagerly. He followed Adams outside and across the street to Tom's Steak House. Thank God he don't favour that Mex food, he thought, a brief grin on his face.

★ ★ ★

Hope Sprague turned the gig in at the rear of the general store. She got down and tied Mike to a post and went up the ramp. She loved shopping even if it were mostly for things Jan had asked her to get for him. He was a hard worker, Hope had to concede. Things weren't half bad since they had bought the house. Months ago, she would never have dreamed she'd be married, living in her own house and shopping for whatever they wanted. Jan had told her, though, not to draw attention by spending too much at once, and not to carry a lot. They always paid cash and mostly kept to themselves.

While Jeff Larson filled her order, Hope poked around the shelves. She was sorely tempted to buy herself a gold chain and locket but, instead, she bought some beads for Alfreda Torres and tobacco for Jaime. They were a real nice couple. She was glad to have them around, especially when Jan took himself off. When he was gone she worried about him. Since becoming his wife she felt closer to him. There was much kindness in him. Perhaps one day they'd have a child but not yet. She could tell Jan didn't want anything to spoil things, not until he'd made more money. He was obsessed with becoming rich. Perhaps he was right, they didn't want to be tied down yet.

Sprague had decided to stay away from town for a while, though he felt sure he had fooled Kreutz, and that he truly believed he'd been robbed by a Mexican. Still, it paid to be careful. He must figure out what his next hit would be. He put the $11,000 into an apple barrel down in the storm cellar. If he ever had to get away in a hurry, it was handy. An amount of $250,000 was what he had in mind to have in his accounts before he retired from his errant ways. Truth was, he enjoyed the thrill of taking from the rich, and some of the not-so-rich. Robbing Kreutz had been the ultimate in pleasure. In any case, $2,000 of the dough had been his own. He whistled cheerfully as he got on with his chores. Working for oneself was a real pleasure. Yes, sir!

★ ★ ★

'I'll pick the stores up later after I've had some coffee,' Hope told Larson, and went on out. She paused to look into a shop window displaying women's winter wear. She was tempted but passed on, and went into a café. She had bought new clothes in Austin, and since she didn't often go out, it would be wasteful to buy more. She ordered coffee and apple pie, and sat dreaming.

When Sam Carver and Buck Adams came out of the steak house, they shook hands. Adams walked off. Sam went into a small store to buy some cigars. He felt like celebrating, but he had to go wash his dirty clothes, and he had to see to his horses at the main livery stable where the stage coaches came in. In the morning he was to check in at the Rangers' office and get his orders. He went on down the sidewalk, a spring in his step. Just as Sam was about to cross an intersection, a gig was coming down the small street. He waited, and when the gig drew abreast, his heart began to thump. The young woman flipping the reins had light-coloured hair dropping on to her shoulders from under the wide-brimmed floppy hat. 'Oh Christ!' he uttered. 'It's her. Hope Bennett.' Then his eyes lit on the horse. Sure as he was standing there, it was his own horse, Mike. His legs felt like giving way as the gig turned into the main street and swept away in a hurry.

131

Pulling himself together, Sam legged it for the livery stable.

He had just got Blaze saddled in a hurry, and was about to mount and go after the gig, when a stage-coach came clattering into the yard. The horses were all lathered up as they came to a skidding halt. The driver was yelling, 'We bin attacked!' He flung himself down from the coach. 'Dan's bin shot! There was three of 'em — Mexicans!'

The ostler and others came running out as the much shaken passengers straggled towards the stageline office. Sam went to help get the dead shotgun guard down off the seat. A moment later Buck Adams came running. 'Well, Carver,' he said. 'Looks like you've got your first job. You might just as well get started today. We can't let the trail grow cold. Haywood is getting a posse ready. If you could get the details from the driver, I'll go get my horse.'

'I'll need more ammo,' Sam yelled at him, as he went off to find the driver. He found him in the line office telling the despatcher about the hold-up.

Hope was shaking like a leaf as she urged Mike along the trail. It was Sam, I know it was! He's alive! What shall I do? He was staring right at his horse. He surely must have recognized him. She eased up a little and looked back up the trail. There was no one following. Tears ran down her cheeks. What shall I do? What shall I say to Jan? Perhaps I could take Mike and leave him at the livery. Of all the times to show up. Pull yourself together, Hope told herself. If only he'd come sooner. She mustn't let Jan know he was here. She was married now. Perhaps Sam was just passing through. But I'm sure he recognized Mike — he'll be trying to find him.

Jan hailed her when she drew up near the barn. 'Did you get the nails?' He was busy building an extension at the end of the barn for the rig and other items.

'I did! I got everything on the list,' Hope said, as she lifted down a box of provisions. 'I've been thinking,' she added as he came to help her, 'it would be nice to go down to see the ocean for Christmas. We need a rest.' She couldn't look at him, and went off to the house. 'I have to go,' she said, flushing.

Jan gave her a quick look, noting her face. Was she perhaps with child? For a moment he felt pleased, then annoyed. It was too soon. He wanted no worries and he wasn't even sure he wanted kids. He and Hope were OK alone. It would be a nuisance right now. He picked up the box of provisions and followed her. In the house he called to her through the bedroom door. 'It'd be a good idea. Corpus Christi isn't all that far. Make a nice change. I'll go to town tomorrow and book seats for next week.' He was thinking there would be plenty of banks there. All those ships coming in — there'd be a lot of money about.

Hope sighed with relief. If they got away for a while, Sam Carver would probably be long gone by the time they returned. He was a bounty-hunter, and they didn't stay long in one place. She would leave Mike in the barn. It was cold anyway. The house was hidden from the trail. It wasn't likely he would come here.

The stage which had been robbed had been *en route* from Austin. It had been carrying a lot of money for the banks. The ranchers had to meet payrolls, and so had the army. A lot of business went on in San Antonio.

They'll be long gone, Sam thought, as he rode with Adams and two other rangers. A small posse had already gone ahead. 'I reckon they'll head south,' Sam said to Adams. 'With all that dough they won't need to rob anybody for a long time. I tell you, $200,000 is one helluva haul!'

'Yeah, well,' said Adams, 'it depends

what sort of men they are. If they stop off in a cantina someplace and get on to the *pulque*, the *putas* will rob them, and their *amigos*, too. I doubt we'll get much back even if we do find them,' he told Sam resignedly. An hour later they were searching the place where the holdup had taken place. They found empty shells, hoofmarks, and dried blood all around. The empty money box they found under some bushes.

After Sam had searched around awhile, he found traces of hoofmarks heading south-east across open land.

'They'll camp somewhere tonight and then probably swing west, and head for El Paso,' one of the possemen opined. 'Too much time has been lost. We'll never find them.'

Haywood was inclined to agree. 'We'll back-track towards Austin a mile or two first. Best if we split up. Two of you head south. Adams and his three will go south-east, and maybe join up with you later. Carver might be following a false trail. There could've

136

been more than three of them outlaws.'

By the time it came dark, Sam still had two sets of hoofmarks in sight, but it was not an easy chore using firebrands so they stopped and made camp under some trees near a water hole that cattle were using. 'How would they know about the money shipment?' he asked Adams.

'Pure chance, more than likely, I'd say. There's shipments all the time, though. Be a good thing when the railtracks come into San Antonio,' Adams replied.

'If one of them is hurt, it might slow them down. They had about six hours start on us, I reckon,' said Sam. 'Might be they'll head for Floresville and hide out among some of their kin. I doubt they'd go east.'

'I'd stake a month's wages on Laredo. That's where a lot of outlaws head for. They can cross over into Mexico quite easily,' said Chas Howard. 'It's a hell of a long way, anything can happen before they reach the border.'

'It sure is,' said Sam, 'and a long way back!' He was thinking of Hope Bennett. She must be living somewhere near San Antonio. Might be working for some rancher's wife. He felt annoyed. Working for the rangers wasn't a whole heap different from bounty-hunting — riding all over the place. Still, he would be paid, and that was something.

★ ★ ★

Nick Kreutz was waiting in the old adobe ruin when he heard the horses coming. A soft whistle came out of the darkness, and he answered it with two of his own. He stood quite still, tensed, his hand on the new Colt he'd been forced to buy after his other one had been taken from him. Since that night he'd been full of anger, and vengeance on his mind.

Carlos Ferrer swung down. He, too, was full of hate. This arrogant gringo, he would kill one day. He would have done it long ago if Kreutz didn't have a hold on him. Unlike José and Pedro, who didn't care, they were being paid as *vaqueros*, and did what Kreutz asked, so long as he paid them well for these extra dangerous missions, and gave them protection. Kreutz had threatened to send Ferrer's family, who lived in Floresville, back to Mexico, and hand him over to the sheriff. He dropped the reins and took the saddle-bags, which he handed over to Kreutz. He snatched at them, then noticing there were only the two of them, and one riderless horse, he snarled at Carlos, 'Where's Pedro?'

'*Pedro es muerto*. The stage-coach guard shot him,' said José. 'He die later, we bury him. Nobody find him.'

Kreutz looked alarmed for a few moments, then he went in behind the adobe wall and stirred the low fire into life. He opened the bags and saw the wads of notes. 'Oh, wow! You counted it?' he asked suspiciously. He knew they would lie, anyway. 'Were you followed?'

'We *vamos* pretty damned quick,' said Ferrer. 'We stop only to bury Pedro. *Mañana*, they will come, *jefe*.'

'Make some coffee while I count it,' Kreutz told him.

Kreutz was quite adept at counting money. When he'd finished, he handed over $2,000 to each of them. Ferrer flushed deeply, and José put a hand to his sidegun, but Carlos moved in front of him. 'I will take Pedro's share for his *madre, por favor*,' he said evenly to Kreutz.

Nick had not missed the exchange between the two of them. He shrugged and counted out some notes. 'Here is a thousand. He should have been more careful. It's a lot of dough for a Mex. You know you couldn't get the information about the shipments. I take risks too. It takes planning. I also protect you. Now, you better be going; stay out at a line shack. I'll be in touch when I got anything else. You've both been on a trip, looking at some bulls over at the Dillon place, *comprende*?'

'*Si, jefe*,' said Ferrer, holding himself in with great control.

'Oh, and you can tell the others, if they ask about Pedro, that he quit.'

The two Mexicans rode away, and Kreutz kicked out the fire. He was grinning widely. $200,000, less what he had paid the bank clerk in Austin, and the two *vaqueros*. A profit of $190,000. Holy Toledo!

Carlos and José rode away towards the Cibola Creek where they parted, one riding northwards up the creek, the other south. Later they left the water where it was heavily ploughed up by cattle hoof-marks. By the time it came light they had both come together again at a line shack on the eastern border of the Lazy K.

★ ★ ★

On the second day, Captain Adams called a halt when he saw a light up ahead. 'It's the Bordens' place. We can sleep in the barn, and I'm sure Jean

141

Borden will let us fix some grub in her kitchen,' he told his men.

The eastern sky was just beginning to show light as the four men, after a quick coffee and ham sandwiches left for them by Jean Borden, rode out to continue their search. By noon, Adams had come upon the adobe ruin. He gave off two shots and the others came riding in. 'It's obvious the ranchhands use this place for branding, and a spot to sleep,' he said.

'I've seen some fresh prints,' Sam told him. 'I'd say someone stopped off here, maybe last night, or the night before, after the robbery.'

'I've seen some hoofprints heading westwards,' Ben Allen interjected.

'I think they might have met someone here,' Adams said. 'There's two sets of prints going due south, only it looks like one horse had no rider, the marks were shallow. There's also others, and they parted near the creek. They're cunning devils.'

'I'd bet on them as went to the

creek,' Jay White opined.

'Well, I was following some marks near the creek, then cattle had trodden all over the place, so I lost them. It could've been a rangeman. I think we ain't going to find 'em now,' Sam said pessimistically.

★ ★ ★

The day after the robbery, Julio Costa, Jaime Torres's nephew, who had taken up residence with the Torres folks, had been to town on his burro. He came back full of the robbery. '*Muchos* dollars! *Tres* Mexicanos, hold up stage. The sheriff, and the rangers, they go after the *bandoleros, señor*,' he spluttered out.

Jan felt himself go hot all over. 'How much *dinero*? Did anyone say?' he asked excitedly.

'*Docientos mil!*' said Julio, his eyes bulging.

'Two hundred thousand dollars,' Alfreda Torres said quickly. She had picked up quite a lot of the gringo language. 'A lot of *dinero, señor*!'

Hope gasped. 'My-oh-my! D'you think they'll catch the bandits?' she asked, then noted the brightness in Jan's eyes. 'They'll get caught one day,' she said.

Jan laughed. 'They'll be long gone. With all that money they can live the rest of their lives in Mexico. No more slaving for the rich,' he said soberly.

'Yes, and they could be shot dead. And dead is for ever,' she said stridently, and went into the house.

The next morning Jan went into town to book seats on the stage for Corpus Christi. He'd been quiet since hearing about the hold-up. Hope saw the warning signals. He's wishing it had been him. Such a haul would have answered his dreams. Why couldn't he be satisfied with what he had?

After paying for the tickets for the stage on Monday, Jan went into the Long View Saloon. He was enjoying a beer at the bar when Nick Kreutz and a tall, lean man came in, and they went to the other end of the bar where the bartender placed two glasses and a whiskey bottle in front of them. Probably his foreman, Jan thought, as he saw that the lean man wore chaps. He studied both of them through the mirror. Kreutz suddenly looked up, and their eyes locked. Kreutz was the first to look away, lifting his glass to gulp down the whiskey.

He recognized me all right, Jan mused. Then it came to him in a flash. His hand shook as he lifted his beer glass. Nick Kreutz was behind the stage holdup. He must have known about the large shipment. He'd probably bribed someone at the bank, either here or in Austin. If only he could make such a haul, Jan thought, enviously. He wondered about the *vaqueros* who'd beaten and robbed him. They probably were hiding on the range somewhere. It had to be them. Why in hell hadn't they just ridden off with the dough? Kreutz must have some hold on them.

They couldn't have known about the shipment.

Jan heard Kreutz laughing, he was knocking back whiskey. Surely Nick got enough dough from his father without having to rob folks? According to that *vaquero*, Kreutz had put a boot into Jan. If he was a heavy gambler, and womanized, that must be his hang-up.

All the way back home, Jan was thinking about the hold-up. When he and Hope came back from Corpus Christi he would try to discover what Nick Kreutz got up to. Might just be he could outsmart that arrogant devil who'd probably never wanted for anything, never had to get his hands dirty at hard labour. By all accounts, Richard Kreutz was a man with plenty of clout in the county, and he'd spoilt young Nick. Well, one day he'd be able to rub shoulders with such as Kreutz, Jan told himself.

# 10

Christmas had come and gone, the weather was flirting with spring. Sam Carver sat in the rangers' office assessing his finances, which now stood at $5,792.50 after he'd purchased a homestead. The three-bedroomed clapboard house not far from the San Antonio River, and within easy reach of Floresville, went with a hundred and twenty acres of land which he had bought from a James Howard, the father of a ranger colleague. Since Howard's wife had recently died he had lost interest in struggling on without her. His son Chas had persuaded him to go and live with his family where he could enjoy seeing his two grandsons. Sam had reason to be pleased and had left the place in the capable hands of a Mexican couple, who had worked for Howard, until he quit the rangers by the end of the year.

During the past three months Sam had covered a lot of terrain, and had made quite a few friends. His mind had often been occupied with thoughts about Hope Bennett. He had made some enquiries after her, but having been so busy he'd discovered nothing of her whereabouts.

The bandits who'd robbed the stage from Austin had got clean away. The bank concerned had not been pleased. Sam and Chas had had some success, however, when they'd ridden down to Floresville to look over the Howard place. On stopping off at a cantina, Sam had recognized three Anglos he had once had a warrant on. He and Chas had followed them to an old shack not far from town, and after some gun-slinging, one outlaw had been shot dead, the other two captured. The reward of $500 on all three had been paid into the rangers' fund.

Recently the rangers had been after a band of cattle rustlers. Richard Kreutz had been to town complaining bitterly at the sheriff's office, and the rangers'. Captain Adams had been forced to give it priority after the Territorial governor had sent him a strong letter. The ranchers had a lot of clout.

Sam put his bank statement away and got to his feet. He'd best be on his way to the Kreutz ranch headquarters and see what could be done. In his opinion, the rustlers would move the cattle at night, probably along dry creek beds and through *malpais*. They would not want the dust to be seen, though in his experience one could smell it. There might be collusion with one or two of the *vaqueros*, he thought. He locked the office door and stood on the board-walk watching a wagon coming down the street. It was the woman's hair that first drew his attention. The sun on it gave it a reddish tint. By God! It was her, Hope Bennett, and there was a fella sitting next to her on the wagon seat, driving the horses. Sam took an immediate dislike to him, as he stood waiting, his heart thumping. When the wagon came abreast of him he stepped out into the street. He took hold of the sorrel's rein, and the horses stopped.

Hope felt herself stiffen, and blood rushed to her face. Sprague called out, 'What the hell you doing?' He yanked the brake on. 'Let go or . . . '

'It's all right, Jan,' Hope said, putting a restraining arm on him. 'Sam, you're alive!' she called out excitedly.

Carver let go of the rein. He looked up at Hope. 'Yeah! I'm alive, and so are you, I see. You ain't got Mike with you today, then?' he said coldly.

'What is this? Who is he?' Jan looked at Hope.

'It's Sam Carver. Remember, I told you about him? How he saved my life. I thought he was dead,' she said, looking strained. 'Oh, Sam! I'm so glad you're not! I have Mike. I'll fetch him in tomorrow. Are you living here, in town?'

'Yep! When I'm not away chasing

outlaws. I'm with the Texas Rangers now. You tell me where you've got Mike, I'll come pick him up. I was real fond of that horse,' Sam answered her, giving Sprague a challenging look.

Sprague leaned across Hope. 'Like my wife said. We — I'll — fetch your horse in tomorrow. I'll leave him at the livery stable where the coaches come in. He's been well looked after,' he said pointedly.

Sam felt as if a cold hand had clutched at his heart. So, she's married, and he be young. Well, I guess that's that. 'What happened to that murdering scum?' he asked Hope, who sat twisting her hands nervously.

Hope hesitated, then said, 'I shot him. Jan found me — he's looked after me,' she stammered.

'Well, I guess that's all right then. You look just fine. You never got to Denver?' Sam said gruffly.

'No, I never did. I'm really glad you're not dead, Sam! I really am,' Hope replied.

Sprague clicked up the horses. 'We're kinda in a hurry,' he said. 'We gotta get on. It looks like rain's coming. Like I said, I'll bring the horse in tomorrow,' he added, somewhat icily. He was remembering how Hope had fretted over Sam. Carver had looked at her real hungry — as if mebbe he'd been stuck on Hope. He wasn't a bad looker, though a few years older. He turned to Hope as they moved on. 'We don't want him out at the house. You'd better stay out of town awhile. We'll be busy anyway, ploughing. He's a ranger now and that could be dangerous for us,' he told her firmly.

Hope said, 'I suppose so,' and lapsed into silence. It had shaken her considerably, talking to Sam again. Her feelings were all mixed up. Sam had looked quite shaken when Jan had said 'my wife'. So, he'd quit the bounty-hunting. She suddenly felt cold inside. Somehow she must talk Jan out of his obsession with getting more money. Surely they had enough now.

*It had been such fun in Corpus Christi over* Christmas and New Year. She had begun to think Jan was settling. She had thought about Sam Carver, though, believing him to be dead until that day she went into town in the gig with Mike. She hadn't been sure, though, if it was him.

Jan had played some poker, and they'd bought each other presents. He had got her the gold locket she'd always wanted, and she'd bought him a fancy waistcoat to go with his new broadcloth suit. They had mixed among the rich folks, staying at a nice hotel where there had been a dinner-dance on New Year's Eve, and they'd had such fun. It had been exciting, especially when the young men had openly admired her, and danced her off her feet. She had even been jealous when the husband-seeking young girls had shown an open interest in Jan. Now clean-shaven, his hair cut properly, he cut a real dashing figure. Two days after the New Year's Eve festivities, Jan had said they must leave. He had dumped the wallets which he had stolen from the drunken young men at the dance down near the wharves. It had been so easy. Jan had learned the art of picking pockets at an early age. It was a game to him and it had excited him enormously to relieve these socializing young bucks of their bulging wallets. He had, however, thought it prudent that they should leave town, as he might just have outstayed his welcome. He told Hope nothing of his haul, though. On the way home, Sprague was already figuring out how he could further enhance his fortunes, and the sooner the better, he thought.

★ ★ ★

After talking with the elder Kreutz and his son Nick, Sam was of the opinion that it was probably Comancheros who were stealing the beeves. They would probably drive them westwards into Arizona, and then sell them to new settlers who would change the brands. Nick Kreutz had firmly dispelled Sam's theory of the *vaqueros* being involved. 'All our men are loyal and have been with us for years,' he'd told Sam. So, he set up his own watch from a ridge. He could see for miles all around. It would be difficult to tell, if he saw cattle moving in a bunch, whether it was Kreutz's rangemen, or rustlers, driving them.

For three days and nights Sam kept a look-out. He rode down to have coffee with the *vaqueros* when he saw a camp fire. He kept alert at night, but he saw nothing to cause him alarm. He packed up and went back to town, where he found a note on a wall-board which told him there'd been a freight-wagon hold-up west of Hondo, and that he should get out there as soon as possible. He stopped only to drink coffee, change his shirt and his horse, picked up some more supplies and rode out again, westwards. As he rode, he thought about Hope Bennett.

Well, she was Mrs Jan Sprague now, and there was nothing he could do about it.

It had not gone unnoticed by two outlaws, Kyle Welsh and Olé Mercer, who'd ridden into town only two days ago, that three deputies from the sheriff's office had ridden out eastwards, in a hurry, then two rangers and then a third, had gone down the westward trail. Sitting on a bench outside a saloon, after watching all the activity, Welsh turned to Mercer, 'Seems to me there ain't but the sheriff left in town. I reckon now would be a durned good time to stick-up one o' them banks,' he said, draining his beer glass.

'Lot of folks about, and some of 'em are well armed,' Mercer replied, spitting liberally. 'Then it could help. Folks ain't keen on shooting when there's so many on the street. First we betta cinch up and take our horses across near the barber's, next to the Mercantile Bank. That's where the ranchers put their dough. We get a good haul, then we ride west and head for Pecos. No posse likes going into that town. They'll figure on us heading for Mexico, most likely.' He expectorated again and got up.

'Yeah, that do make sense. We do it quick. It ain't long until closing time, the drawers will be full. Come on! Let's do it!' said Welsh.

Jan Sprague had just come out of a locksmith's and was about to go quench his thirst at the Long View Saloon. Might even take a hand in a poker game, he was thinking, as he crossed the street. He was midway when the two men came charging out of the Mercantile Bank. A shot rang out from the pistol of a man in the bank doorway, one of the robbers turned and fired back, the man ducked back inside. The other robber was on to his horse, yelling for his pal to hurry.

Jan, who had run to the boardwalk, pulled out his Colt and fired at the fleeing men, one riding a black, the other a roan. Jan's shot missed, and he sought cover in a doorway as a bullet plunked into the wall. People were scattering in all directions, into doorways, behind wagons, or whatever shelter they could find.

The sheriff came out of his office, and Jan shouted to him, 'The bank's been robbed,' and then ran to get his roan. A minute later he was galloping after the two robbers, who had turned down a side street. By the time Jan got out into the open, he was a good half mile behind. It would do no harm for his status, he was thinking, if he could capture those two outlaws, and there would probably be a price on them. Way behind he could see a buckskin coming. It came to him then that the man in the bank doorway had been Nick Kreutz. He urged Nippy on and began to close the gap between him and the outlaws. Suddenly, one of them veered, weaving in and out of thick bush, and then went down into a dry-wash, out of Jan's sight.

Nick Kreutz was coming fast. He had been in the bank when Welsh and Mercer had drawn their weapons, telling the customers to lie face down on the floor. One of them had tossed a bag to a teller, yelling at him to fill it quickly. Mercer had grabbed a woman, putting an arm around her throat, threatening to choke her if they didn't comply. Nick had tried to pull his colt but Welsh had stepped on his arm, and kicked his piece away, then bent down and taken Nick's wallet, into which he had just placed $500. He'd been first to the doorway and fired a shot at the fleeing figures. He'd heard Sprague shout, seen him run for his horse. It had made him angry. Of late, he had a growing suspicion that Sprague was not all he appeared to be. If he was a young prospector, he'd eat his hat. What was there to mine around San Antonio? What if he was actually helping those men to get away? He holstered his Colt and drew out the rifle from under the saddle flap. It was rather confusing with two men riding roans. He saw one in the far distance leave the trail. The black was already out of sight. One of them fired at Sprague when he came up from a hollow. He obviously missed.

Kreutz turned to look back and saw the sheriff and two other riders coming at a hand-gallop. It had also occurred to him that there might be a reward. He was livid about losing the $500. Lately, he had lost over $30,000 to some cattle buyers from Chicago. His pa was on his back about the rustling. He suddenly remembered that Ferrer had told him about being robbed by a gringo. It seemed strange, an Anglo robbing a Mex — they had little, unless Sprague had figured out about the night he was robbed at the Blue Bonnet. Nick put spurs to the buckskin, in a rage.

Sprague had also taken out his rifle, and suddenly he hauled in, lifted it and took careful aim at the rider of the black horse as he came out of the draw. He squeezed the trigger, Welsh fell forward over the horse's neck, it slowed, then went on again as Welsh managed to pull himself up. He slapped the horse with the reins and it ran on.

Mercer had stopped near some rocks and took a shot at Kreutz, who hauled in quickly, unsure about where the shot had come from. He looked back, saw Sheriff Haywood coming over a crest, some way back. His gaze then fell upon a rider who'd just come from behind some rocks, then another on the black. They set off hurriedly, and suddenly came together, one having difficulty staying in the saddle. Sprague must have hit the fella on the black, Kreutz thought. The man appeared to be passing something to his accomplice, who took off quickly heading back to the drywash.

The exchange between the two had also been observed by Jan Sprague. He could see the rider on the black was about finished, and Nick Kreutz would soon catch up to him, and the others. He could see that the wash turned to the south some 300 yards ahead, so he took a chance and cut the corner — coming to it, he hoped, way ahead of the outlaw, who he figured would be using it for cover. When he came to the rim Jan steered Nippy down behind some mesquite. It wasn't long before a stone rattled, and a sagehen flew up. Jan stepped down, putting a hand to Nippy's muzzle. It had gone very quiet. Sprague stood as quietly as an Indian, hoping that Kreutz wouldn't come tearing along and spoil things. Most likely he had waited for the sheriff to catch up, and claim he had shot the outlaw. Nippy's ears went forward, his nostrils quivered as the other roan came along the wash. Jan let it go past then ran down and, snatching a rein, he stepped back and put his rifle up into Mercer's back. 'Don't move, don't turn round. Just sit quiet. Throw the pistol to the ground, then throw the bag hanging on the pommel to the ground also. Do it now, there's others coming. Do as I say, I'll give you your life,' Jan said crisply, prodding Mercer again.

Mercer was shaking. How in hell had the bastard got in front of him? He dropped the pistol, tensing. If he could just leap off the horse . . .

'Your life for the dough,' Jan repeated. 'Hurry! It's the best deal you'll get. It won't bother me none to shoot you now, there's still the reward.' He knew quite well he couldn't shoot the man in the back.

Mercer lifted the bag and dropped it near Jan's feet. Jan dropped the rein, hit the horse hard on the rump and it leapt forward, running hard along the wash and was soon gone out of sight round a bend, Mercer trying desperately to gather up the reins and stay in the saddle.

Jan picked up the bag quickly, got back to Nippy and was into the saddle. He ran Nippy up the other side of the wash and into the *malpais*, loping hurriedly until he came to the old dead cottonwood that was hollow inside. He tossed the bag into it and kept on going, sweat clinging to his back, a smug grin on his face. When he had gone some yards further, he suddenly jerked a rein and threw Nippy over. He only just got his leg out of the way in time. He hated doing this to the horse, but he had to make it look good. He fired two shots into the air as he lay beside the horse. It wasn't long before Kreutz and Phil Carmody, a top hand at the Harden ranch, came tearing to a halt. Jan had got his boot off, and was sitting up.

'What the hell happened to you?' Carmody enquired.

'You might well ask,' said Jan. 'The horse went over. I guess I'm lucky my leg ain't broke.' He put on a good show of agony, holding his foot.

'Where's that thieving bastard?' Kreutz asked angrily.

'I took some shots at him. I must've

missed. I know I hit the other one. Did you catch him?'

'Yeah, Sheriff Haywood and Jack Samms have him. I doubt he'll last long. He's lost a lot of blood,' Carmody told Jan.

'He had only a few bucks on him,' Kreutz snarled. He was lying, though. He had found the $500 which Welsh had taken off him in the bank, before Carmody had caught up. He was looking hard at Sprague. 'Christ! We have all these lawmen, and rangers, and two men can just walk in like that and rob the bank. That other fella must have the dough,' he said crossly.

'Well, most of the deputies and rangers were out of town chasing after other outlaws,' Carmody said.

'Maybe them two were tipped off,' Kreutz replied. 'There's been a lot of robberies lately.' He was looking hard at Jan who was pulling on his boot, and wincing.

'Well, I'd advise you not to use the Blue Bonnet. It's mighty dark in that street — so I found to my cost,' Jan said bitterly, giving Kreutz a hard look. Kreutz turned away, and mounted his horse.

Jan, too, mounted. He would have to tread warily around that one. He had the killer instinct in him, if he didn't guess wrong. The three of them rode on back to where Haywood and Samms were standing over Welsh, who had just expired.

'Well, that's one we don't need to waste tax-payers' money on,' Haywood said. 'What happened to you?' He looked at Jan, who had dust and earth on his jacket.

'My horse fell, or I'd have had that other one. I shot this one, though,' he said pointedly. 'Will you be going on?'

'I guess we'll have to, if he's got the dough,' said Haywood resignedly. 'I hope you're willing, Jack.'

'Sure, I'll go. Anybody else?' Samms said.

Nobody responded so Haywood and

Samms got mounted. 'You'll take the body in, Phil? Or you, Sprague? You'll get the reward if there is one, once we find out who he is — was.'

'I'm taking his horse, his guns and what's on him,' Kreutz butted in. 'He took $500 off me. I guess he gave it to the other fella.'

'You can't do that, Nick. There'll be the undertaker to pay, and the stiff might have relatives somewhere,' Haywood said sharply, and turned and rode off.

Kreutz went red, and swore. He looked at the other two. 'I'm going home. You do what you want,' he snarled, and put his spurs into his horse.

'That kid sure has a mean temper,' Carmody commented, pulling out the makings. 'His pappy sure done spoilt him.' He and Jan tied the dead man on to his horse then headed back to the trail.

'Kreutz is no boy,' Jan opined.

'His ma lost two kids, so they made

a lot of fuss over Nick. Time he got married, but I doubt he'd settle until he gets the womanizing outta him, and the boozing and gambling,' Carmody prophesied.

# 11

Jan spent the next few days at home, helping to plant corn and vegetable seeds. Hope could see he was in an agitated frame of mind, all tensed up. He'd told them about his part in chasing the outlaws, making little of it. Jaime Torres's cousin, Manuel, on a visit from town, said he'd heard Nick Kreutz say, 'Señor Sprague should have caught the other bandit. Maybe he let him go, he say. Nick plenty drunk in the Long View Saloon.'

'If I hadn't got off quick after them, they wouldn't have got one,' Jan said scathingly. Kreutz was sure trying to make trouble for him. Sounds as if he's got a guilty conscience about something, Jan thought.

The next evening, Jan went into town where he got into a poker game at the Long View Saloon. About nine o'clock Nick Kreutz arrived and got into another game with some young ranching friends, a banker's son and a visitor from back East. Jan wasn't playing serious poker, none of the players at his table could afford the amounts seen at the other table. He had other things on his mind, though he was not unaware of how things went in the other game. Kreutz had won a fair pot, and was calling for more whiskey, making a lot of noise. Jan threw in his hand. 'I can't concentrate tonight,' he apologized. 'I guess I'll be off home.'

'If'n I had a wife like yourn, I'd not be leaving her fer long,' said Etham Jolly, chuckling.

Jan just smiled, and said 'Goodnight!' He went out quickly and got on to Nippy and rode down the street as if on his way home. After he was well away into the darkness he swung off the trail heading south, riding carefully across flat open land for about two miles before he turned westwards. It was at an old buffalo wallow that he drew rein and sat under some trees. Would Kreutz be coming, or would he send his *vaqueros*? He had got away quickly from the saloon. He could be mistaken, though his instincts were seldom wrong. He would have to share the dough with Kreutz. No, that would put him in to Kreutz's hands. He could not afford to let him know. He was only suspicious, and Haywood had no liking for Kreutz, that Jan knew. He could never let anyone know about his other life. Hope was coming round, she liked the good life. They would leave San Antonio, especially now Carver lived there. He was no contest, though; he had only a small homestead, he would never have much. Hope wouldn't want that kind of life now. Carver's imagination didn't stretch too far. Hope, he smiled, had bought a book on how to behave in polite circles. She was teaching him to write and spell better. He thought some of the ranchers ought to read that book. Most of them were nobodies, really. Nippy paddled. 'Easy boy,' Jan whispered, and slid his hand to his Colt.

A bit jangled and a horse snorted some yards away. He could hear them talking. Two at least. Perhaps they were *vaqueros* who had been into town. Kreutz's men. He slid his pistol out, and he patted Nippy. 'Stay quiet,' he told him. The horses went on by, but Jan stayed where he was for quite some time. Changing his course, he went northwards, often stopping to listen. It was only a matter of some ten miles to the dry-wash, but he must not let anyone follow him there. He couldn't tell if the riders were after him, or had simply been on their way somewhere. Then why not take the trail? Jan was good at losing any followers, he'd had plenty of practice. He had familiarized himself with much of the terrain since coming to San Antonio. He had noted the hollow cottonwood tree when he had gone looking for the Mexicans who had robbed him. Were they still working for Kreutz, he wondered?

Although it felt cold, Jan was sweating inside his shirt. He had no idea how much dough was in that bag. It had felt heavy. The bank had not given out how much they had lost, perhaps they didn't even know. He rode a wide loop to the west, reminding himself that the bandit might also still be around. What if he had caught a glimpse of him that day? What if he'd seen Jan throw the bag into that tree? What if it wasn't there? His stomach turned over and he urged Nippy on.

An hour later, Sprague arrived close to the drywash and was south of the dead tree which stuck up grotesquely against the night sky. The night was fairly dark as the moon was waning. Jan went down into the wash and dismounted, leaving Nippy tied firmly to a bush. Then taking his rifle and an axe, he went quickly up over the rim. He ran crouched, using the brush for cover. When he came to the dead tree, he knelt down and for some time he listened. A coyote howled not too far off. Another answered to the south. Jan relaxed a little and tapped at the bole. It was hollow all the way down. He thought it had probably been struck by lightning some time ago. He felt at the base and prised away quite a lot of dead wood. With luck he might not need the axe. Sounds carried a long way in the night. He placed a glove over the end of the handle and struck the tree bole hard. The handle went inwards and he drew it out excitedly, thrusting his hand in. He found his glove and a lot of rotted wood. 'Oh hell!' he said. Then he thrust his arm upwards and found something stuck up there. He worked the pulp away with his hand and suddenly the bag fell down. Cold sweat ran off the end of Jan's nose as he yanked the bag out. Quickly, he picked up the glove, the axe and his rifle, and ran back to the wash. He rammed the bag and axe into the bedroll tied on the cantle, and tied up the end. Then very quickly he cut a piece of brush and went back over his tracks, to blot out his footprints. He rode away with his pistol in hand, ready. Inside he was all uptight. He longed for a shot of whiskey, but he kept on going across land where many cattle moved about.

The dawn was showing in the east as Jan rode along the trail for Austin. He had changed his mind about taking the stage from town. It was too risky. He would leave his horse at Braunfels and get a stage from there.

When he believed it was safe to stop, and having put a lot of miles behind him, Jan went into a café at a settlement and ordered a large breakfast. Hope would be worried, he thought. Then she was used to his going off. Maybe she wouldn't have to worry for much longer.

When he arrived at Braunfels, Jan had missed the stage so he put Nippy into the livery stable, paying the ostler for a week. He then got a room at the hotel. After he'd locked the door he opened the bedroll and took out the money-bag. Most of the money lay as it had been thrown in. There was a mixture of notes and a few silver dollars. Jan smiled. It was better than wads of new notes. He put it all back into the bag and then into a saddle-bag, then after a wash-down got into bed.

He was awakened next morning by boots clumping along the corridor and got up leisurely. It was about eight o'clock when the stage-coach arrived for Austin and he got aboard.

About eight days later, Sprague stepped off Nippy in front of his barn. Hope came striding across, her face showing the fury she felt. 'I've been worried sick,' she told Jan. 'Nobody has seen you since you left the Long View Saloon, when you said you were going home. It isn't good enough! My nerves are shot to pieces,' she snapped at him, flushing.

Jan took the saddle and bridle off the horse and let him into the corral.

Determinedly he hung the gear up, and turned to Hope. 'We'll discuss this in the house,' he said tersely. 'You ought to know by now I have to go off sometimes. I hadn't time to come and tell you. I didn't want that young show-off, Nick Kreutz, nosing into my affairs.' He strode off towards the house.

Hope followed him through up to the bedroom and shut the door so that Alfreda Torres couldn't hear them rowing. 'Well, Nick Kreutz has had plenty to say about you in town. There's a thousand dollars reward on that man. Sam Carver knew him, he once had a warranty on him. His name was Welsh, I think.'

'I see, so dear old Sam is back in town,' Jan said angrily. 'Perhaps I should make it clear to him, you're my wife now.'

'For heaven's sake, don't change the subject. Just where did you go to? One of these days you'll be killed and I won't know what's happened to you,'

Hope said tremulously, pulling out her handkerchief.

'Aw, hon, don't get into a frazzle. I went to Austin to see about my affairs. I went to see a lawyer. An' I saw some real nice houses. We should move up there. You would like it, there's more to do.'

'How could you look at houses without me?' Hope sniffled. 'I like it here. The railroad will come soon.'

'Look, everything I do is for you, for us,' Jan told her, putting an arm around her.

'I just wish you would tell me when you are going off. I feel such a fool. Even the Torreses are beginning to wonder. They never got that other robber, nor the money. For God's sake, Jan. I never know what you are up to. We have a good life now, don't spoil it.'

Jan got out of his clothes and into bed. His head ached, his body was weary from tension and riding.

Hope went out and then came back

with a cup of coffee. Why couldn't Jan be more like Sam? She didn't really want to move again. She felt settled now. This was her first real home since she was a small child. How long would it be, if they moved to Austin, before Jan wanted to move again?

Sprague sat up, taking the coffee. 'Hey, how much dough did the bank lose?' he asked offhandedly.

'Oh, I think it was ahout fifty thousand. They hadn't counted it, but a lot of folks are real mad, especially Nick Kreutz. He says they took five hundred dollars from him that the teller had just given him.'

'Yeah, I know. He said he was taking that dead man's horse and gear.'

'Sam says he can't have them, as the man had a brother in Wichita. He gets what there is after the undertaker is paid, so I understand.'

Jan laughed harshly. 'Kreutz still has money to play poker with his wealthy pals. One of these days he'll have to mortgage the ranch, I shouldn't wonder,' he said.

'You be careful of him, Jan. He's mean, nasty,' Hope told him. She didn't tell him how Kreutz had made up to her in the general store.

Sprague lay back, smiling. After he had counted the money in the bag, it had amounted to $57,300. He had put that into one of his accounts, all but $5,000, which he had paid into the Wells Fargo Bank. It was better that Hope didn't know about it. She might just let something slip to Carver. Oh God! It had been one of the sweetest jobs he had ever pulled. Possibly the best. No one could have done it better. He lay chuckling to himself. One more good hit and he was through with it. Hope was right. One day his luck could run out.

# 12

Jan Sprague was feeling in good humour as he reined in his horse at a tie-rail. The first person he saw coming down the boardwalk was Sam Carver who called out, 'Howdy!'

Jan responded likewise, rather coolly. 'You have any luck finding that bank robber yet?' he asked Carver.

'Nope. I reckon he's down into Mexico or Arizona by now. We lost track of him,' Sam responded.

'He'll probably lie low. With all that dough he don't need to rob again, I reckon,' Jan opined.

'True,' said Sam. 'Oh, thanks for bringing back my horse. I'm kinda fond of Mike. Hope keeping well?' Sam lingered, regarding Sprague closely.

'She's fine. I'll tell her you were asking,' said Jan and moved on. Carver always made him feel uneasy. He had a way of looking at him, making him feel guilty.

Carver watched Sprague walk away. He sure would like to know the story on him and Hope. She seemed very nervous whenever they met up. Just how did Sprague make his dough? Sam doubted the few acres he owned would produce much. After hearing some of Kreutz's comments, he had been thinking real hard. Had Sprague helped that bandit get away? One day while riding up the trail a young Mexican had come out from a track. He'd told Sam about the Torreses and that they lived about half a mile away, and were working for Señor Sprague. A few pertinent questions had come up with a few answers that had intrigued Sam. He had also discovered where the Spragues lived. The youngster had mentioned how the *señor* went looking for gold; that he was a prospector. Sam had lain awake that night jogging his memory about certain robberies that had taken place in New Mexico and then at Abilene. The description of the lone robber had been vague. Youngish, not tall, not small. Long, light-coloured hair, and a beard. Jan Sprague was clean shaven, his hair cut short. But he might have had it cut since he came to San Antonio. In fact, now he recalled, the land agent mentioned that Sprague had a beard when he'd bought the house, when Sam, after running into Hope and Jan, had been to see if he could find out where they lived. Then he'd had to go out of town the next day for some time.

Just how had Hope gotten away from that Lew fella, he wondered? She said she had shot him. He couldn't see such a hardened outlaw letting her get at his guns. It might be she was covering for Sprague. Why? Sprague wasn't over-friendly. Might be he was jealous. He was young, a good-looking fella. He seemed to have dough, though the property, being run-down, hadn't cost much by all accounts. It was easy to see why Hope would take to him. Perhaps she didn't care how he made his dough. Sprague had probably had a life similar to hers. They were likened spirits. I sure as hell don't want to be the one to take him in one day, if he is the lone bandit, Sam thought, as he went into the rangers' office.

★ ★ ★

Sprague went into the sheriff's office to enquire whether the reward money on Kyle Welsh had come through. Haywood was getting up from his chair. 'Ah! Sprague! I've got a bank draft for you. Just go along to the National Bank and they'll give you the dough.'

Jan grinned. 'I hear the other fella hasn't been caught. If my horse hadn't gone down on me, I'd have had him, too. If Kreutz hadn't stopped, so might he. He sure is a mean-tempered son-of-a-gun.'

'Yeah, Nick's a hot-head. His pappy

should rein him in some,' Haywood responded.

After Jan had collected the $1,000 from the bank, he went straight to the general store and purchased a bottle each of whiskey and brandy, and two of good wine. Then he selected a nice gold bracelet for Hope, a box of cigars, and lastly, some prime steak. Tonight, they would celebrate. As he rode home his mind dwelt on his next robbery. It would be his last. The adrenalin flowed through his body, as excitement took him over.

* * *

One thing Sprague had taken note of while he was down in Corpus Christi was the amount of freight that got transported on the huge wagons, after being discharged from the coastal and Caribbean ships. It was a risky business. The Comancheros to the west often robbed and killed the teamsters. In a matter of a few years the railroads would have a network across the country. He and Hope would have a real fine time, they could go and take a look at this great land.

'I wish you wouldn't go off,' Hope beseeched him. 'I have a bad feeling.'

'Aw, Hope! Don't take on so. After I've done this trip we'll go up to Austin and have us some fun. We'll go look at houses. It's too dull here. You know what to do if anything should happen to me. Go to Austin, take the dough and go back East. You could change your name. You have the address of the lawyer, he'll help you. There's enough for you to live comfortable for the rest of your life. 'Sides, nothing's going to happen to me. You take care now,' Sprague told her, and stepped on to the roan.

\* \* \*

Two days later Sam Carver rode into the yard. Hope was hoeing up some potato plants. How she loved helping

186

to make things grow. She looked up from her chore as the Torreses' dog started snapping and snarling at Sam. Although she was pleased to see him, a sense of foreboding came over her, then guilt. 'Sam, it's good to see you!' she called to him, and yelled at the dog.

'I was passing, so I thought I'd call in,' Sam explained, his colour heightening.

'I should have asked you over for a meal,' Hope apologized. 'You seem to be away so much.'

'Yep, that's a ranger's life. I'll be quitting come the end of the year. I have my own place to run now,' said Sam. 'You on your own?' He gazed around him.

'Oh, Jan's away. He went someplace looking for minerals. He has a thing about finding gold, especially after he's been talking with old-timers,' Hope said, not meeting Sam's eyes.

'You don't seem to be in bad shape here. I'm glad you ended up all right. I looked for you for quite a long time, but I never found any trace of you. I was worried what the murdering devil might do to you,' Sam said, following her into the house.

'Oh, Daggett! He got too smart for himself. I had to kill him. I'm sure he intended to kill me after he'd had his fun. Jan helped me to sell the wagon, and the spare horses. I couldn't part with Mike and Will's horse. It's so good to be free, Sam. I never had a home before. Not since we left England and I don't really remember that. I'll go make some coffee,' Hope said, and went off to the kitchen. 'You can tell me all about the rangers,' she called back to him.

★ ★ ★

The big freight wagons were all loaded up, and the heavy-set teamster in charge rode up to the front wagon. 'Let 'em roll!' he called to the bearded man who waited, reins in hand. Sitting next to him was his eighteen-year-old

188

son, thin, wiry and tense, a shotgun on his lap. 'Relax, Billy,' Tim Higgins told him. He whipped up the team of eight mules which strained at the harness and set off with the load of spices, sugar, rum, bolts of cloth and hardware items awaited by the stores and trading posts.

Jan Sprague sat in a café watching the last wagon pull out. He was on the east side of the huge bay into which ran the Nueces River. Maybe he should get into freighting. No, it was a risky thing, and he would need a helluva lot more dough than he had, just to buy the wagons, and pay the men. Having $200,000 in the bank at one per cent was better. He might, one day, put some dough into a store. Anyway, me and Hope are going to have some fun, once I've done what I have to do. He paid for the meal and left, walking over to a small Mercantile Bank which was a branch of the main one in Corpus Christi. He walked up to a barred counter, pushed two $100 notes

189

under it to a middle-aged, balding man wearing steel-framed glasses. 'I'd like those changed to tens,' he said, glancing around the small room.

The man counted out the notes and slid them to Jan, who placed them into his wallet. 'You must get plenty of dough in here, all that freight business,' he said affably.

'Most hauliers pay by cheque at the main bank,' the thin-lipped teller responded. 'They have them new type safes with dial locks.' He pulled out a timepiece from his vest pocket. 'We'll be closing now,' he said.

Jan said, 'Time surely moves on, don't it?' He left the bank, and strolled back to the rooming-house where he'd taken a room. There were many such small harbours along the coast. Galveston, further up, was about the largest port. At a half after six Jan got off his bed and went to the waterfront for his evening meal. He ordered the choice of the day, fresh fish. It was almost eight o'clock when he went into the Square Rigger Tavern. Most of the men inside were seafarers off the ships in the harbour, and a few old locals who scrounged drinks off these hard-drinking mariners. Few had firearms, but most carried knives, hidden about their person.

Jan noticed a card game in process at a corner table. He sipped his beer, debating the wisdom of joining in with such men, though they did seem to be taking the game seriously and quietly. He decided against it, his mind on other matters. He went back to his room and lay on the bed again. He had already paid for the room and had told the proprietor he would be leaving very early heading for Kingsville. It was after midnight when he took his gear and went downstairs. An elderly nightwatchman slept soundly in a chair, as Jan slipped past the office. He let himself out and headed for the livery stable, a quarter of a mile away. There, too, the night ostler was sleeping soundly. Jan saddled Nippy, and led him out. The street was dark and full of holes. The natives of Gregory had been abed long ago, and all was quiet. Some time later Jan arrived at a warehouse across from the small bank. He tied Nippy under a lean-to used by customers. 'Stay quiet,' he said, petting the horse.

During the day Jan had taken note of a windowless one-storey building adjoining the bank. This he figured was the office and probably where the safe was kept. He had also seen an unbarred window on the second floor of the bank, unlike the one below at the front. In seconds he had climbed up a drainpipe and landed on the flat roof of the adjoining building. Very quickly he had the window open, which was rotting from the seawater squalls. Inside he struck a match, shielding it with his hands. He crossed the room between some stacked crates, opened the door leading to a landing and went down a spiral staircase into a passage. First, he opened a door that led into the bank's service area, and closing it again, he cursed as a match burnt his fingers. He carefully scooped up the burnt-out remains and put them into his pocket. Lighting a fresh one he then opened another door and stepped into a small room where he saw a lamp on a desk. He got it lit and surveyed the room. It was windowless. Besides the desk, there were two padlocked cupboards, and a metal cabinet. Drawing a screwdriver from his pocket he undid the hasps on both cupboards. There was nothing inside but files, ledgers and boxes of paper, some rubber stamps, and at the bottom of one, some rubber boots. Jan cursed again. Perhaps he was wasting his time. It'd be a hell of a thing if he got caught and there was nothing worth stealing.

He started on the metal cabinet, but the hasps were forged in. From his pocket he drew out a bunch of keys he had had for some years. One by one he tried them until a larger one seemed to almost fit. He turned it slowly, then all at once the lock was open. Pulling back the door, his eyes lit up. *Dinero!* Dough! He pulled a bag from inside his coat and started filling it. There wasn't a lot, but it was a nice little haul. Looking up to the top shelf, he gasped. Oh wow! Gold bars!

There was no way he could take it all, and even if he had a wagon, it would take time hauling it up and out through that window, then down. Someone might see him. He took six bars weighing probably about two pounds each. He placed them into a hessian sack he found on the shelf. Working feverishly, he locked up the cupboards again, then put out the lamp. The money-bag he pushed inside his coat, the sack he carried in one hand while holding a match in the other. He had to stop twice to light fresh ones before he reached the window. He couldn't get the latch back where it had been so he had to leave it. He reached the ground in a hurry and went across to the horse, putting a hand on its muzzle. He put three gold bars into each saddle-bag, and the money-bag. He swung up into the saddle and pointed Nippy away from the warehouse, heading for some tall reeds a couple of hundred yards away. He figured it to be about two o'clock as he rode along a track used by local fishermen, and animals. It was wet and squelchy, the hoofprints filled as the horse went on. An hour later, Jan saw a sign pointing north-east; someone had shot away the name of the town. Jan took the trail, he was heading more or less in the direction he wanted to go. Before it came light he was camped in a hollow hidden by bushes. He must have covered about twenty miles or so. It had been rough going and he was tired. He took his bedroll off the horse and covered himself with a blanket after placing his rifle and the saddle-bags next to him.

The rain awoke Jan, and he sat up hurriedly. He pulled out his timepiece and saw it was almost nine o'clock.

Damn it, he'd stayed longer than he'd meant to. It was possible that the bank might open early, to accommodate the shipping companies. It would take some time to notify the sheriff, when the robbery was discovered. There was no reason why he should be a suspect, but any stranger in town would be remembered, especially by the old timers who sat around. A bright sheriff might go to the rooming-house to check on who had been there and left. His leaving early would draw attention, though no one would know just how early. He'd given a false name. They'd never find his tracks. Still, he must get on and put more miles behind him. The rain abated as he rode up the trail at a steady lope. He passed one or two Mexicans on burros. It would be likely that the seamen would be prime suspects, Jan thought. When he saw a town of fair size up ahead he chose to avoid it, and eventually landed up in a small settlement, mostly full of Mexicans and one or two rangemen. He drew up at a poor-looking shack which was both store and cantina. The big, black-haired woman behind a rough counter looked him over hopefully.

'I'd like some food, if you have some,' Jan said, smiling.

'*Si señor*, I make. I bring,' she said, pointing to a bench outside.

Jan sat down, wearily. His thoughts were on the dough. He still hadn't counted it. The gold bars would fetch a nice bit, but he didn't know the price of gold now. He would have to go to Austin to dispose of it. As he figured it, it would be a three-day ride to where he could leave Nippy and get a stage. He would not use Braunfels this time. The woman brought a bowl of chilli beans and bread. It wasn't his favourite but would have to do. 'A bottle of tequila,' he told her, and handed her two dollars.

# 13

Nick Kreutz was in a foul mood as he entered the cantina at the edge of Floresville, which he'd often visited with Ferrer. That Ferrer and his sister and his family were gone was no real surprise. Ferrer's sister had meant nothing to him, he'd just used her, given her the odd present. No one would say where they had gone to. He ordered tequila, feeling the resentment around him. These Mexicans kept sheep and goats, though some worked on the ranches. He had wasted a whole day and still had a long ride back home. His money from the stage robbery was dwindling fast and he owed money to a friend, who'd told him he'd better pay up or he would ask Nick's father for it.

He took the bottle and sat at a table waiting for some food to be brought to him. His bad mood had been brought on mainly because of Jan Sprague, whom he had seen heading south across Lazy K land three days ago. He had followed Sprague but lost sight of him when it came dark. That strutting coyote was one sly critter. Him and his good-looking wife were something of a mystery. She sure kept herself out of touch. She never joined any of the women's committees and such. Real haughty! By god! It'd be something if he could take her away from Sprague. One day the Lazy K would be his, and then he would enjoy the rewards. He would need a wife to get him some sons. He finished the stew the woman had put in front of him, took another long drink of tequila, and was about to get up and leave when José Canaris came in. He looked startled when he heard Kreutz's voice. '*Como estas*, José?' asked Nick, pulling a dollar from his pocket for the meal.

The *vaquero* in Kreutz's employ

turned red. '*Jefe*, I was over on the west range. The *segundo*, he say . . . '

'It's OK,' said Kreutz 'Have some tequila.' He sat down again, the *vaquero* joining him. A lot of eyes turned their way. Nick told the woman to bring some more food for Canaris. He plied him with tequila, but discovered nothing about Ferrer, as Canaris was as much in the dark as Nick. Feeling frustrated, Nick got up. He opened his mouth to say something to the *vaquero* and just at that moment two Anglos walked in through the door. Kreutz froze, and turned his back to them, whispering something into Canaris's ear.

Mercer did not notice Kreutz as he called for a bottle of brandy, which the sour-looking barman lifted off a shelf and placed on the rough bar with two glasses. The two Anglos moved to a table near the door and were soon deep in conversation.

A few moments later Canaris got up

and sauntered to the open doorway, followed by Kreutz. At the doorway, Canaris turned and seized the smaller of the two men while Kreutz, who had his Colt in his hand behind his leg, lifted it suddenly and hit Mercer on his head, and he slumped across the table. The other one, taken completely by surprise, spluttered out, 'What the hell!'

'Don't move, *señor*, or I make the leetle accident,' Canaris told him.

The barman came round from behind his bar. '*Que pasa aqui?*' he said angrily.

'This man is wanted,' said Kreutz. 'And him too, most likely. Now we're taking them out of here, so don't interfere.'

The barman returned behind the bar, muttering, 'Damn the gringos.'

Canaris hoisted up the smaller man and dragged him outside, while Kreutz got Mercer to his feet, who was still rather groggy. 'Where are you taking us?' he asked. 'Who are you? Wadya want? We ain't done nothing!' he said innocently.

A black and a brown horse stood at a tie-rail across the street. Very quickly Canaris had his man's wrists tied and then slung him over the brown horse.

Mercer was trying to make a break for it, and Kreutz hit him again. He got him tied onto the black horse, one he remembered from the chase. 'Go get our horses,' he told Canaris, a nasty grin on his face.

★ ★ ★

Kreutz, leading the black horse, and Canaris, leading the brown, were loping steadily for San Antonio some thirty miles away when they decided to stop and rest. They made a fire in a hollow, took out the bottle of tequila and sat drinking. Their two prisoners sat glowering, their backs to a fallen tree bole, Mercer complaining about his head, which bore a nasty gash above his right ear. 'Why have you got us tied up like this? Like I said, we ain't done nothing,' he told Kreutz.

'I know well enough who you are,' snarled Kreutz. 'You're the one who took my $500 in that bank raid. You'd better tell me where all that dough is the two of you got away with. Well, Welsh sure as hell didn't have it, so you must have it. What's left!'

'Christ, I ain't got it! One of your thieving lawmen took it. Didn't he turn it in?. He told me 'the dough for your life', so I reckon you got nothing on me, nor him.' Mercer looked at his sidekick.

The sidekick, whose name was Ben Rickman, said, 'Olé ain't got much dough. We've both been looking for work. So you'd better let us go. We done nothing. I sure as hell don't know nothing about a bank robbery.'

Kreutz laughed. He looked at Mercer. 'I never saw anyone catch up with you. Your pal was shot. He died. He had but a few bucks on him, so you had the dough. You've got it hid somewhere.'

'You go to hell. I gave it to that lawman. You better ask him, whoever he was. I'd sure like to catch up with him. I never saw his face. Hey, you a bounty-hunter?' Mercer asked Kreutz.

'Hell, no!' said Kreutz. 'Well, I guess there must be a warrant out on you two, and we can claim the reward.'

Rickman was shivering, and wishing he had never met up with Mercer. Maybe he did have the dough stashed someplace. He wasn't much for talking about himself.

★ ★ ★

Sheriff Haywood was at his desk drinking coffee when Kreutz and Canaris pushed the two outlaws into the jailhouse. He got up hurriedly. 'Nick, what the devil . . . ?'

'I got that bank robber. He says his name is Olé Mercer, and he don't have the dough. I reckon there must be a dodger on his sidekick, his name's Ben Rickman. Mercer, here, says a lawman

204

took the money off him. Didn't I tell you, Sprague had time to get to him before we found him on the ground. He could've thrown that horse himself.'

'There'll be a trial,' said Haywood, pushing the two men into a cell. 'It'll all be gone into.' He was thinking the bank directors wouldn't be too pleased that no dough had been recovered. It did seem strange.

'I'm telling you, Sprague has the dough. You should go search his place,' Kreutz demanded, red in the face.

'You better be careful, Nick, what you say. I'll have to think this over.' His mind was already thinking thoughts he didn't want to deal with.

Kreutz and Canaris went to a café to get a decent meal. Kreutz was protesting loudly about Haywood.

'This Sprague you mention. He go find Carlos, he take *dinero*. He hit him hard,' Canaris told Nick.

Kreutz looked thunderous. 'I don't know how that bastard knows so much,' he said bitterly.

'*Quien sabe!*' said Canaris, shrugging. If he got half the reward for the two men they had just taken in, he would *vamos* like Carlos had done. He had no liking for Kreutz, who spat on the Mexicans, but used their women.

After questioning Mercer at some length, Haywood was of the opinion that Kreutz might have a point. There was little known about Sprague, though he remembered that Sam Carver had known Sprague's wife before he came to San Antonio. The Spragues seemed to be a respectable couple, then sometimes the quiet ones were full of surprises. He would have to go talk with Sprague and get his version. He certainly had shot Welsh, and then his horse had stepped in a hole and thrown him. Both Kreutz and Sprague had been out of his sight for some time before he'd caught up to Kreutz and the dying Welsh. If Mercer had got the money, he'd not have been hanging around this area, surely. It was possible he knew quite well who had taken the dough off him, and was awaiting his chance to get at Jan, when he saw him. It might have been Kreutz who'd taken the dough off Welsh, and stashed it someplace. Nick was not above doing such a thing, He was an inveterate liar, and he went through dough like it was water. Perhaps Mercer had been trying to blackmail Nick. Who knew what had been going on? Haywood didn't fancy tangling with Nick's father, that was for sure.

He went through and had a talk with Ben Rickman. He had no warrant on him. He had no real cause to hold him. He insisted that he'd run into Mercer only a week ago. Mercer said this was a fact, so he was forced to let Rickman go. As soon as he was free, Rickman left town in a hurry. Later that evening Haywood found Sam Carver in the Long View Saloon, and asked him about Sprague. Sam was non-committal. He did not tell Haywood of his own suspicions, his thoughts were on Hope. If Sprague had taken that dough, then he was a thief, and if Hope knew, it, she could be in plenty of trouble, might even go to jail. Sprague certainly would, if anything could be proven. Oh Lord, if only he hadn't let that fella Daggett make such a fool out of him, Sam thought.

Nick Kreutz was fuming. He felt certain that Mercer knew who had taken the dough from him. Sprague could have promised him a share, and gone back on his word. Anything was possible. Mercer would not know his name nor where he lived. That's why he'd stayed in the area. If Haywood brought Sprague to the jailhouse and let Mercer see him, and promised him he'd get a lighter jail term, he might tell the truth. He might say it was Sprague just to get the deal. Kreutz grinned. Somehow he would fix that smug devil. Haywood couldn't refuse to go fetch Sprague, if his pa were to tell him to. His job depended on the ranchers who voted him in.

By the time Jan Sprague reached Austin he was exhausted. He'd taken five days to get there. His roan had gone suddenly lame at a place called Lockhart, and with regret he had sold him and taken the stage. The homesteader had promised he would rest Nippy until he recovered, and had taken Jan into town on his wagon.

He had taken a room at a hotel he knew, and slept for several hours. It had not taken him long to dispose of the gold bars, which were not marked, to a goldsmith who asked no questions and gave him a fair price. He deposited all the money he had with him into the accounts he'd set up, then went to see his lawyer, C. B. Grant, leaving a letter with his will in a sealed envelope with him. Jan's entire fortune would go to Hope should anything happen to him. Once they had moved from San Antonio it would be better for them both. They might even go abroad for a spell, like a lot of the rich folks did. The next day he boarded the stage for Braunfels, where he purchased a fresh horse and headed on homewards in a relaxed frame of mind.

After Sam Carver had ridden out to tell Hope that Nick Kreutz had brought in Olé Mercer and that he was making accusations against Jan, she was sick with worry. She had denied, vehemently, that Jan would have done such a thing. Indeed she knew nothing about it. Jan had just claimed the reward on Welsh.

Sam had looked worried, though. What if Jan had been that foolish. He had told her he was finished with it all. Where was he now? What was he up to? That small pick and old map he carried would fool no one who knew mining. Why couldn't he be satisfied? There was only a nominal amount in the account in town. Most of Jan's money was in Austin. Why should anyone be suspicious? Well, if anyone should ask about their affairs, she'd say his pa had left him plenty.

Hope sprang up from the bed when she heard the soft whistling. She rushed out as she heard the back door opening. 'Sorry, hon! I didn't mean to be gone so long,' Jan explained apologetically. 'I got lost.'

Hope stood looking at him strangely, then she burst into tears. 'Where have you been? What have you been up to? The sheriff is coming to see you. Sam's been! They've caught that robber. Welsh's partner,' she said hysterically.

'Woa, take it easy. Let's get some coffee,' he said, his pulse quickening. What the hell had that fella gone and told them?

Hope made the coffee, while Jan deposited his gear and rifle into a cupboard. 'Now start at the beginning. Why did Carver come out here?' he said calmly, though his stomach was fluttering.

'The man's name is Mercer. Nick and one of his *vaqueros* saw him in

211

a cantina, somewhere south. Mercer swears he gave the money-bag to a lawman who let him go. Kreutz says it must have been you, as you were the only one way ahead, and he had stopped to apprehend Welsh.'

Jan spoke angrily, 'He would say that. It could have been him. They know my horse threw me. I've had to sell Nippy, he went lame on me.'

'Oh, no!' said Hope.

'What does Carver think?' Jan asked her, controlling himself. The less Hope knew the better. No one could force anything out of her then. He would stick to his story. That Mercer fella had not seen his face, he knew.

'Sam doesn't like Nick Kreutz, but I think he's suspicious. He was asking where you were, and where we were before coming here. I don't think he will say anything to Sheriff Haywood, though,' Hope replied.

Jan poured himself a whiskey. 'Well, I've got nothing to hide, they can search this place. They can't prove a thing. We'll move out of here soon. There's too many lawmen and rangers, always looking to arrest folks. Back East they have trains, and boats down the rivers. We can have ourselves a real good time. We deserve it. You're smart, and as soon as I can read and write proper, well, we can do as we please.'

Hope smiled through her tears. 'Oh, Jan, let's do it. I can't stand being scared all the time. I'm afraid you'll get caught.'

'I'm definitely finished with all that. I've been to Austin, and I've seen that lawyer. I've got his card and I want you to keep it somewhere safe, just in case. There's a letter and my will. You hear me?'

Hope took the card Jan handed to her. She went and put it away in her private box where she kept the gold items which Jan had bought for her, and a brooch that had belonged to Helen Morris.

The following afternoon Sheriff

Haywood showed up. He was quite formal, Hope noticed. He went into the kitchen for coffee, at Hope's invitation. Jan followed. He had seen Haywood arrive and had walked over from the barn. Haywood got right down to it. 'I want you to come to town and identify the robber, Olé Mercer,' he said, looking at Jan keenly. 'He claims a lawman, he thinks, took the bag of dough from him, and let him ride off.'

Jan was prepared, and was calm. 'Sheriff, if you think I have the dough, you are welcome to search the house and buildings, and see my bank balance at the National Bank. I can't identify this Mercer fella. I never saw his face. Kreutz did. He saw both of them, he was in the bank at the time, and they took his $500.'

Haywood smiled. 'If you did take the dough, you could have hidden it anywhere. You've had plenty of time since that day. Like I said, I'd be obliged if you'd come and take a look at the fella. I'm not accusing you of anything,' Haywood said evenly, and got up.

'I'll do that, Sheriff, first thing in the morning. I've got a sick cow to tend to,' Jan said, barely holding his temper.

'It might be that you can get the fella to own up and say he took it. The bank's on my back. They're mad as hell we got the robbers but no dough.'

Haywood went out and got mounted. 'Thanks for the coffee, ma'am,' he told Hope.

'I'll see Jan gets off early in the morning,' Hope called pleasantly. 'He's tired today, he's been to Austin to see about a house; we are thinking of moving up there. It's too quiet here, and I get lonely. I need to see a doctor about my chest, too,' she added, as Haywood turned to ride off.

'Why in hell did you tell him that?' Jan exploded as they went back into the house.

'Because I don't want anyone putting it around that we cleared off in a hurry. It might look bad,' she said.

'You've got a smart head on your shoulders, hon! I reckon that's what attracted me to you,' he said, and swept her off her feet.

★ ★ ★

Haywood was in the jailhouse doorway as Jan rode up next morning. 'I see you've got a fresh horse,' he said.

Jan looked the sheriff right in the eye. 'Yes, I had to sell the roan, he went lame on me. He's got a good home. He'll be looked after,' he said evenly. Haywood don't miss a thing, Jan was thinking as he followed him inside. 'We probably won't need horses in Austin. The bay is oldish, I'll give him to Torres when we do leave,' Jan told Haywood.

'Too bad you done all that work on the place, and then you're leaving so soon.' He poured some coffee and handed a mugful to Jan. He was playing for time, hoping Sprague might show signs of guilt, perhaps. He really didn't think Sprague had taken the dough, he believed it was a story Mercer had concocted after he had gotten away, in the event he should ever get caught. These outlaws were plenty resourceful.

As they exchanged pleasantries, Deputy Larry Wiley suddenly came in looking anxious. 'I got a telegraph from Corpus Christi,' he said. 'There's been a robbery!'

Haywood snapped at Wiley, 'I can't do nothing now. It ain't in my jurisdiction, anyway. What the hell's the matter with them down there?' He got up from his chair. 'Come on, Sprague, let's get this over.'

Jan got up, relieved. For a moment he'd felt sick. It did seem odd though, sending a telegraph to San Antonio, and more than a week since he'd robbed that bank. He stepped forward as Haywood led him to the cell, where

217

Mercer sat smoking a cigarette.

'As I told you, Sheriff,' Jan said: 'I never did see the man's face. He wore a grey overcoat, as I recall.'

Mercer got up and stood glaring at Sprague, but kept silent. He knew the voice all right.

'I'm sorry, Sheriff. I can't say this is the man. I'd be lying if I said he was. I never saw his face as I was chasing him. He looked round once, but he was too far off. He did ride a roan horse, that is all I can say.'

Mercer was somewhat confused since Kreutz had been to see him. Kreutz had been hinting at something, as if he wanted it to be this fella, who he now knew was no lawman, to be arrested. Well, why in hell should he help a rancher's son. This fella knew well enough it was him, he felt sure, whom he'd taken the dough off. Well, now he knew for sure who had the dough, and if he stayed quiet, they might give him a short sentence, and then he'd find Sprague. He said nothing, and they left him to dwell on his thoughts.

'Listen, Sheriff,' Jan told Haywood, 'I was chasing both robbers. Kreutz was way behind. I eventually got a shot at the one on the black horse. He rode on awhile and actually came together with the other man, and something was passed between them. The roan ran down into a wash. I saw Kreutz coming up fast as the black horse's rider fell over its neck. I ran into a lot of rough and the horse must've hit a hole or something and went over. I barely managed to get my leg out of the way. You know what happened next. You and Samms came along.'

'You were out of sight for some time, though, when you were down in the wash,' Haywood interjected.

'Sure, I was after the roan, and he went up again.'

'Well, Mercer ain't saying nothing. Kreutz says you were out of his sight for some time, and me and Samms and Carmody were too far back to see what was happening. Kreutz says

219

he ain't sure now about this fella,' Haywood, said frustratedly. He went back to the cell.

'Mercer, we got a dodger on you for a robbery in Lubbock. The judge would go easy on you if you told us where you've hid the dough. I reckon you couldn't have spent it that quick,' Haywood tried again.

'Kyle had the dough,' Mercer said, changing his story. 'That fella is telling the truth. I reckon Kyle dropped it someplace, hoping to go back for it, before he took that bullet. I ain't saying no more.'

Utterly fed up with the whole thing, Haywood went back to his desk and sat down. 'I'll need you at the trial to testify, it's on Monday at ten o'clock,' he told Jan. 'Just say your piece like you told me. Unless you can think of something else.'

'I'll be there,' said Jan. He walked out of the office and went to find Hope, who had come in with Alfreda Torres in the gig. He found them in a tea shop. 'I'm going to see the property agent and tell him we want to sell up. You finish your shopping then we'll go on home. I've had enough of this place,' he said.

After Haywood had read the telegraph from Corpus Christi about the robbery at the small branch bank, he noted a description of a youngish man, darkish hair and several days' growth on his face. He put the telegraph into a drawer. For a moment he wondered. Sprague had been in Austin looking at property, and could probably prove it. There were plenty of youngish men who might have done the robbery. 'I'm going home for my dinner, you look after things,' he told Wiley.

# 14

It was almost midday by the time Jan Spraque gave his evidence at the trial. Mercer stuck to his story, insisting that Kyle Welsh had taken the money-bag from him, and that he must have dropped it someplace. The lawyer appointed by the Council couldn't budge him. Nick Kreutz was emphatic that Welsh, when he caught up to him, had not had the bag. Sprague was up front, he must have seen what went on between them. He could have picked it up. Sprague sprang up, protesting.

In the end, the lawyer led the jury to bring in a verdict of robbery, but there was no proof of where the money had ended up. Mercer got two years for his part in the hold-up. He was also to be transported to Lubbock to face other charges in connection with a robbery there three months ago.

Kreutz was fit to be tied. Sprague had gotten away with it. He felt certain he had taken the money, and had it stashed somewhere safe. He had heard the rumour about the Spragues selling up and leaving town. He was certain now that Spraque had posed as the Mexican to hold him up on the trail, at which time he lost $11,000. That prissy wife of his was probably in on it. He went straight to the Long View Saloon and asked for a bottle of whiskey.

Jan and Hope went for a meal, inviting the property agent to join them. He told them, 'Since you've made the repairs to the house and buildings, I see no reason for it not to sell quickly. Speculators are snapping up as much land as they can. The railroad will soon be here.'

'Well, that's good news,' Jan said. 'I'll send you our address as soon as we get settled. I'd like the Torreses to stay on, and hope that whoever buys the place will employ them. They are good reliable folks.'

Nick Kreutz had been drinking hard, and was still shouting off at the mouth as Jan and Hope were preparing to leave town in the gig. He caught sight of them and shouted out to Sprague, 'You been spending my dough, Sprague, on that wife of yours? Buying her lots of fancy do-dads!' He was weaving about and suddenly he pulled his Colt out.

'Take no notice of him,' said Hope. 'He's drunk!'

Just at that moment Sam Carver had ridden into town, after a futile chase trying to catch two horse-thieves. He tied Mike to a rail and walked over to join the Spragues. Several pedestrians had stopped to stare at Kreutz, who was spinning his Colt on a finger. Two aged women shook their heads in disapproval.

'Where you got it stashed?' Kreutz shouted again.

Sprague, his face set hard, stepped away from Hope. 'Take care of her, Carver,' he said from the corner of his mouth.

'Stay here,' said Sam, to Jan. 'I'll sort him out.'

Sheriff Haywood and Phil Carmody had come out of the jailhouse and saw Kreutz. 'Oh hell! That damned young fool,' said Haywood. 'Nick, you put that gun away afore you hurt somebody.'

'He's got the dough, I know it. How much did he pay you, Sheriff?' Kreutz shouted, his face muscles working, saliva dripping from his mouth.

Jan undid his holster flap. 'You'd better go home, Kreutz. Someone might be putting two an' two together. That coach robbery, your *vaqueros*! That night at the Blue Bonnet when I was robbed and beaten. They were your *vaqueros*,' he called out to Kreutz.

There was a hush on the street, more people had come out to stand in doorways, exchanging shocked glances, and suddenly were chattering among themselves.

Kreutz went purple with rage. 'You lying bastard, Sprague!' He lifted his

Colt and squeezed off a shot. Hope screamed as Jan staggered. Kreutz fired again. Then a tall rangeman stepped forward and hauled him back. 'You fool! For Christ's sake, they'll hang you,' said Harris, the Lazy K ramrod.

'He was going to shoot me, it was self-defence,' Kreutz snarled, pulling away. Then suddenly scared, be rammed his Colt into its holster, as Haywood came striding over.

Sprague lay still as Hope got to him. Blood was already seeping through his shirt. 'Oh, Jan!' she wailed and pulled him up into her arms.

Sam Carver came and knelt beside her, and saw Sprague lift his head and look at her. 'It was all for you. I sure did love you. Remember, the lawyer,' he said feebly as blood poured from his mouth, and then he died.

Sobbing uncontrollably, Hope whispered, 'Dead is for ever! Didn't I tell you?'

\* \* \*

It was Sam Carver who saw to things, arranging the funeral. He stood by Hope's side, along with the Torreses. Several tradesfolk attended, and Sheriff Haywood. Most of them remembered the Spragues as quiet and polite, people who had always paid cash for their purchases. There had been a lot of conjecture about Sprague's insinuations, and those of Kreutz.

Kreutz's father had ridden into town as soon as he got word his son was locked up. The ramrod, and a couple of *vaqueros* who had not actually witnessed the shooting, swore that Sprague had drawn first on Nick. Haywood was forced to let him go, though it stuck in his craw. Even Carver's version was not enough against the three, and that of one of Nick's friends who had come forth. He had been drinking with Nick, and his parents were churchgoing, respected folks.

Two weeks after Jan Sprague's untimely demise, Hope had herself well in control. Alfreda Torres had been a tower of strength and helped Hope through her grief. Sam Carver tried his best to get her to stay on, but failed. 'It's too quiet here on my own,' Hope told him. 'When I get settled I'll write to you. I'll find work,' she assured him.

Hope left Jan's clothes with the Torreses, and gave them the wagon and horses. To Julio she gave the bay which was ageing, and a rifle that had belonged to Lew Daggett. To Sam she gave the sorrel and saddle, and let him take some tools. Everything else was to be sold. The Torreses drove her to town on the wagon which carried her belongings in two trunks. She also took Jan's saddle and bedroll with the rifle tucked inside.

Sam was there to see her on to the stage, while the Torreses stood weeping copiously. The *señor* and *señora* had been like family to them, they told Sam.

As soon as the stage-coach got under

way, Hope sat back and closed her eyes. Another chapter of her life had gone by; she made a vow to herself then and quietly relaxed.

* * *

The night was cool, the air filled with a fragrance of sage, as Hope sat waiting on the horse she had purchased. It was now Saturday, or possibly Sunday, she thought. For two days she had watched the trail from the Lazy K, hoping to see Nick Kreutz riding along it. Across her lap was Jan's Winchester, cleaned, levered and ready. His old bedroll was tied at the cantle. She had often used the rifle to kill antelope. She was a good shot. Hope had felt bitter that Kreutz had walked away free. Just when Jan had given up his robbing ways (which she knew he had enjoyed, really, as if it was a game), Nick Kreutz had to take his life. Kreutz was worse than Jan. He'd never wanted for anything. He was vicious, spiteful and very vindictive. Perhaps it was a fool thing she was about to do. Well, if he didn't show before daylight, she would have to let it go. What if she were to get caught? She'd made a vow, she should keep it. She missed Jan more than she could bear, and she was almost certain now that she carried his child. He would have grumbled when she told him, then been proud. He'd had a poor life as a child, the same as her. They'd never been children in the real sense. Nick Kreutz would never have been hungry, never gone without, and his pa had probably never even smacked him. Damn him to hell! A tear slid down Hope's face, as she pulled out Jan's silver timepiece, struck a match, shielding it under her jacket. It was two o'clock. She wasn't even sure if Kreutz had gone to town, though he might have ridden in another way across the range. He seldom missed Saturday evenings. He'd probably be shacked up with a whore somewhere. She got down and stamped her feet, and went to sit on a small boulder, pulled out a small cheroot, a habit she had formed lately, and lit it, again hiding the match.

A coyote sent a mournful howl across the plain, and Hope sat up with a start. She had dozed off. There was a faint hint of light in the east. Damn it! Had she missed Kreutz? She smiled. If Jan could see her now. She sat a while longer, deliberating, then suddenly she heard a horse coming along the trail. She saw the buckskin as she waited tensely at the side of the cottonwood. Her stomach turned over. She took a grip on herself. Kreutz was actually humming to himself. Hope stepped out. 'Kreutz,' she called out clearly.

Nick Kreutz reined in, cursing. 'What the hell?' It sounded like a female. 'Who's there?' he called back apprehensively. He was about to draw his Colt when Hope fired.

'For Jan!' Hope called back to him. Then she fired twice more into his chest. Kreutz slid from the saddle, the horse shot off down the trail as Hope slapped it on its rump. She went to Kreutz and bent over him as he lay on his back. 'You!' he said barely above a whisper, as he stared up at her in shock. Hope smiled, but not with her eyes. 'Yes, me! You murdering piece of scum.'

Kreutz died then, still staring at her. She put a hand to his neck for a moment, then she walked away.

When she got on to the horse she was shaking, near to retching. She lit up another cheroot, then rode away. By the time she reached Braunfels it was late afternoon. She had entered the Austin trail two miles northwards, after riding along a dried-up creek bed, and then ridden back down the trail. If anyone did trace the tracks to the trail, they would not be able to tell which way she had gone, there was plenty of traffic moving over it. She had learned a lot from Jan about covering their trail. She went to the rooming-house where she had taken a room, explaining that she was going to visit friends at a homestead for a few days, and slept until next morning. After partaking of a large breakfast, she collected her carpet-bag and her horse, and rode leisurely to Austin. She got a room at a small hotel, and asked them to send for her trunks which would be waiting at the stage-line office.

That very afternoon she went to the law firm that Jan had told her about, and asked for a Mr C.B. Grant. Hope had never liked to display her feelings, but she put on a good display as the distraught widow. She did not wish Cecil Grant to think there had been any foul play about her husband's demise, at least not on her part.

Cecil Grant offered his condolences. 'So young to die,' he said, solicitously' as he took the death certificate. 'Shot, I see,' he said.

'Yes,' said Hope. 'He never had a chance. The man was drunk. He got away with it, claimed it was self-defence,' she told Grant.

Grant went to a cabinet and fetched

out a large envelope, and handed it to Hope. 'Your husband's will. I will see it gets attended to as quickly as possible. Do you need any money?' he asked.

'No, not at the moment,' said Hope. 'I don't know how much my husband had. His father left him some. Our house and land will be sold, in San Antonio. There'll be something from that.'

'Well, your husband left everything to you. I believe he has three accounts here in Austin. Just tell me where you will be staying, Mrs Sprague, and I will be in touch with you, as soon as I've contacted them.'

Hope gave Grant the hotel's address and Grant showed her out. She got back to her hotel in a hurry and took out the will, and the letter that Jan had left with it.

Two days later, Cecil Grant came to the hotel and gave her the details of the accounts. She was visibly shaken. After Grant had left, she went downstairs and asked for a bottle of brandy.

She'd had no idea of the amount Jan had accumulated. Back upstairs she sat sipping her brandy. There was more than $200,000, which Jan had said was his aim. But how had he got it? She had known about some of it, and he'd told her he'd won at poker. Her suspicions grew as the day went on. Oh lawks! Had Kreutz been right about that money from the bank in San Antonio, which was never recovered? The hell with Kreutz — that's probably where he is. Poor Jan, to give it all up, then to get killed by that creature. She had always been afraid it would happen. My God! I'm rich, Hope giggled, as the brandy took hold. She got undressed and into bed, feeling emotionally and physically exhausted.

★ ★ ★

The news that Nick Kreutz had been found shot dead, on the trail, hit the streets rapidly after two *vaqueros*, who'd found his horse browsing, then the body, had ridden into town with Nick across the saddle. There was a great deal of speculation and conjecture, as rumours buzzed in the saloons, since Nick's wallet hadn't been taken.

Sam Carver took the news philosophically. 'Was sure to happen one day. His folks'll be broken up though,' he told Buck Adams.

Adams sighed. He'd just received Sam's resignation. 'I sure wish you would do me one more favour. Go see if you can find any trace of hoofmarks and so on. Old man Kreutz is putting up $2,000 reward.'

'Then there'll be no chance now of finding anything. Bounty-hunters and others will have been all over the ground. Haywood followed some hoofmarks, but lost them, so I understand. I'll go take a look, though.'

'You heard anything from the widow, yet?' Adams asked.

'Naw, I doubt she'll write. The

property has been sold. Well, I'll be on my way then,' Sam said, covering his embarrassment.

★ ★ ★

The ground was soft from overnight rain. Sam located the spot where Kreutz's body had been found. There were plenty of bootmarks all about, just as he expected. He scouted about on both sides of the track. From all accounts the shooter had been up fairly close. He went to poke around by some cottonwoods, and came across a small butt from a cheroot. He immediately thought, it was probably a Mexican. Then he saw some smallish footprints. Odd, he thought, they looked as if a woman's small boot had made them. Some Mexican fellas had small feet. He doubted some whore would come out here and lay for Kreutz. Anyway, whoever had done it had known just where to put the bullets.

Sam found some hoofmarks almost

a mile from the trail and followed them until he came to an old creek bed. Just as the sheriff had done, he lost any further sign of the horse's tracks, and came to the trail. He loped on back to town in a confused frame of mind. Kreutz probably had had enemies. A thought still rankled, though. Supposing . . . ? Hell no, Hope had no horse. She'd taken a saddle and a bedroll. Could've got off the stage. Could've had a rifle in that bedroll. She'd killed Daggett, hadn't she? He went and put Mike away and then bought a bottle of whiskey, before he went up to the hay-loft and proceeded to get drunk. He woke up at the sound of buckets rattling, with a thundering headache.

# 15

When Sam Carver walked into the store-cum-post-office in Floresville, the buxom woman weighing out flour for a customer called out, 'Morning, Sam' I'll be with you in a minute.'

Sam left a list on the counter. 'I'll come back later,' he told her. Madge Rodgers, a widow in her thirties, had made it clear she was available to Sam. In fact, he was constantly on her mind since she'd first laid eyes on him over a year ago.

'There's a letter for you,' she yelled, dumped the bag of flour and took the envelope to him.

Sam took it eagerly, trying to mask his excitement. There was only one person from whom he ever expected to get a letter. He went quickly over to Jacques Lamont's bar and ordered a whiskey. His hands shook as he opened the strong envelope. Something dropped to the floor and he scooped it up quickly. It was a photograph, and as he stood staring at it he saw a woman seated on a chair, a child on her lap. He swallowed down the drink and called for another, then went to a table and drew out the letter from the envelope.

*Dearest Sam*

*I'm sorry I haven't written before this, but I've had a busy year. As you will see from the address, I landed back in Vicksburg at the orphanage. In fact, I am running it. We have fifty young children, none older than twelve. First thing I did was dismiss all but three of the staff. Truth is, Sam, I bought the place. I live in my own house in the grounds. Young Jan was born last March. He is such a joy. If only his father could be here too. He'd be so proud.*

*Before I left Austin, I read in a San Antonio newspaper that Nick*

*Kreutz was found dead on the trail. I guess he got what he deserved. Well, je ne regrette rien. I do hope you are enjoying your life and all goes well with the animals. I think I was not really suited for farming. I am contented with my life here now. I wish the Morrises could see the changes. I did learn a lot from them which is useful.*

*Take care, Sam, and have a good Christmas and a prosperous New Year. If you should get over this way, you know where to find me. Please, do write.*

*With our love, Hope and little Jan.*

Very carefully, Sam put the photograph and letter into the envelope and placed it in his inner pocket. A moment later, he pulled the letter out again and went to the bar where Jacques Lamont gave him a strange look. Sam usually drank beer. 'Jacques, take a look at them words, ain't they French?' he asked showing the phrase in question to Lamont.

Lamont put on his steel-framed glasses and read the words. 'Sure, it says, I have no regret. You know, nothing to regret.'

'Yeah, I see,' said Sam, and put the letter back with the photo. 'I'll take the bottle,' he told the smiling Lamont, who had smelled a whiff of perfume on that letter. Lamont had been a trapper, a buffalo-hunter on the Llana Estacardo, and had scouted for the army before opening up a trading post around which Floresville had evolved. Poor Madge, he was thinking, as he watched Sam hurry out the door.

Sam picked up his order from Madge Rodgers and went on home, where he worked up a sweat chopping logs until it was time to feed the hens and two hogs. His helper Manuel Cordez attended to the milking, while Juanita, his wife, cooked the supper. As soon as she had gone to their adobe, Sam poured himself a large whiskey and sat before the fire. He took out Hope's letter and the picture, which he sat staring at awhile. After he had finished reading the letter again, he suddenly sat up straight. 'By God! She did it. She shot Nick Kreutz! She's got no regret. She's telling me,' Sam told himself.

Sprague, he must have left her a hell of a lot of dough. How else could she buy up an orphanage and look after fifty kids? Damn it! Sprague must have been the lone bandit, and he must have got that dough off Mercer, like Kreutz said. Sam finished the whiskey and poured out another large amount. He remembered something Hope had said, just as he'd died. 'Dead is for ever.' That's what she said. He lifted the glass. 'Jan Sprague, if you can hear me. That dough has sure been put to good use. And Amen to that! Well, here's luck to you, Hope,' said Sam, and drained the glass. Laughing out loud, he poured the glass full again.

# RIDERS OF RIFLE RANGE
## Wade Hamilton

Veterinarian Jeff Jones did not like open warfare — but it was there on Scrub Pine grass. When he diagnosed a sick bull on the Endicott ranch as having the contagious blackleg disease, he got involved in the warfare — whether he liked it or not!

# BEAR PAW
## Nevada Carter

Austin Dailey traded two cows to a pair of Indians for a bay horse, which subsequently disappeared. Tracks led to a secret hideout of fugitive Indians — and cattle thieves. Indians and stockmen co-operated against the rustlers. But it was Pale Woman who acted as interpreter between her people and the rangemen.

## THE WEST WITCH
### Lance Howard

Detective Quinton Hilcrest journeys west, seeking the Black Hood Bandits' lost fortune. Within hours of arriving in Hags Bend, he is fighting for his life, ensnared with a beautiful outcast the town claims is a witch! Can he save the young woman from the angry mob?

## GUNS OF THE PONY EXPRESS
### T. M. Dolan

Rich Zennor joined the Pony Express venture at the start, as second-in-command to tough Denning Hartman. But Zennor had the problems of Hartman believing that they had crossed trails in the past, and the fact that he was strongly attached to Hartman's Indian girl, Conchita.

# BLACK JO OF THE PECOS
## Jeff Blaine

Nobody knew where Black Josephine Callard came from or whither she returned. Deputy U.S. Marshal Frank Haggard would have to exercise all his cunning and ability to stay alive before he could defeat her highly successful gang and solve the mystery.

# RIDE FOR YOUR LIFE
## Johnny Mack Bride

They rode west, hoping for a new start. Then they met another broken-down casualty of war, and he had a plan that might deliver them from despair. But the only men who would attempt it would be the truly brave — or the desperate. They were both.

## THE NIGHTHAWK
### Charles Burnham

While John Baxter sat looking at the ruin that arsonists had made of his log house, a stranger rode into the yard. Baxter and Walt Showalter partnered up and re-built the house. But when it was dynamited, they struck back — and all hell broke loose.

## MAVERICK PREACHER
### M. Duggan

Clay Purnell was hopeful that his posting to Capra would be peaceable enough. However, on his very first day in town he rode into trouble. Although loath to use his .45, Clay found he had little choice — and his likeness to a notorious bank robber didn't help either!

# SIXGUN SHOWDOWN
## Art Flynn

After years as a lawman elsewhere, Dan Herrick returned to his old Arizona stamping ground to find that nesters were being driven from their homesteads by ruthless ranchers. Before putting away his gun once and for all, Dan forced a bloody and decisive showdown.

# RIDE LIKE THE DEVIL!
## Sam Gort

Ben Trunch arrived back on the Big T only to find that land-grabbing was in progress. He confronted Luke Fletcher, saloon-keeper and town boss, with what was happening, and was immediately forced to ride for his life. But he got the chance to put it all right in the end.

# SLOW WOLF AND DAN FOX:
## Larry & Stretch
### Marshall Grover

The deck was stacked against an innocent man. Larry Valentine played detective, and his investigation propelled the Texas Trouble-Shooters into a gun-blazing fight to the finish.

# BRANAGAN'S LAW
### Emerson Dawn

To Angus Flint, the valley was his domain and he didn't want any new settlers. But Texas Ranger Jim Branagan had other ideas. Could he put an end to Flint's tyranny for good?

# THE DEVIL RODE A PINTO
## Bret Rey

When a settler is cut to ribbons in a frenzied attack, Texas Ranger Sam Buck learns that the killer is Rufus Berry, known as The Devil. Sam stiffens his resolve to kill or capture Berry and break up his gang.